The Sun Sets in the West

George R. Blake

Table of Contents

Chapter 1: 1959

I don't know what I would have done differently on that day in 1959. Looking back—or is it ahead? I am old and my mind is not as sharp as it was—I know that an unusual alignment of the sun with a black hole caused a nuclear reaction at a laboratory in the mountains of Los Angeles, affecting the lives of a young couple for whom I was employed. It might be said that the position of that day's sun made it possible to change the world.

It was the end of the 1950s. The Nazis had been defeated, the Soviets, who had not, were on the march. The country's postwar boom was coming to a close, as the culture shifted from the *Saturday Evening Post* to *Playboy*. The White Sox were in the World Series. A Communist dictator was throwing a tantrum to go to Disneyland. There was no Medicare, no Amtrak and no Homeland Security. There was also no Viagra, Bluetooth or iTunes. The United States was putting military advisers in Vietnam while striving to put a man on the moon. Civilization was heading for a climax, giving way to something sinister, or to something grand, or to something in between—as if an unknown evil creature was slithering around the globe while the world was turning toward lasting peace and prosperity. We were firing rockets into outer space and listening to rock and roll.

As an educated man with roots in Europe, I'd come to America armed with an acquired sense of skepticism—if you've been to Europe, you understand why—paired with a tendency toward gloom. I was jolted by American innocence. I sensed an imminent danger when I arrived. I wanted to make it stop, to be on the side of good.

I have to admit that I had no idea where to begin. I would learn much, much later that there are men who know where to begin.

THE
SUN SETS
IN THE WEST

GEORGE R. BLAKE

Working for Dr. and Mrs. Thurman seemed like a safe haven. As an assistant to Theodore Thurman, summoning the energy to go to work every day, my duties were frankly menial: setting up experiments, filing papers, scheduling appointments. As a boy, I had wanted to be an artist. As a man, I was catering to a repressed scientist.

He was brilliant, no doubt about it. Having attended the finest universities, I was perfectly disposed to assist him. When I was hired, I assumed that I would help the physics professor complete his studies and that the job would last no more than several months. The work was complicated yet purposeful. Dr. Theodore Thurman studied furiously and wrote voluminously about the principles of physics, making notes, developing theories, forming hypotheses—then, presenting papers, delivering lectures and responding with detailed explanations. I was there for every step. There would not have been a progression without me. I know that my disciplined assistance helped the physicist.

Dr. Thurman's assignments were simple yet demanding. He would labor for hours, fall asleep at his desk, wake and start again, producing an application and immediately commencing another dictation for another course of study, finishing just before sundown in a furious nonstop outpouring of theories and equations. I'd be there to grab a pencil, flip a stenography tablet and pick up some new train of thought. Mostly, the dictations led to dead ends, though at the time they often seemed full of possibility. Mrs. Thurman, who was quite pregnant, usually occupied herself by walking with one of the ranch hand's wives along nearby dirt trails, reading alone in the library or whistling while working in the kitchen. She wisely stayed out of her husband's wild-eyed work and steered herself clear of his way.

I thought the work would eventually end when his various notions were exhausted or ran their course. But there was always another idea, followed by another experiment. Each one seemed more important than the last.

It was as if Dr. Thurman, as I addressed him, thought he might have been circling the possibility of a logical progression which would lead to some singularly groundbreaking discovery, though he certainly never discussed such prospects during our daily encounters. Looking back on those years now, I recall that he generally was immersed in the study of applied physics at that quiet, Western style California ranch house overlooking the valley, where he worked as his wife read, strolled, cooked, cleaned and managed the multi-acre property. There I was, drawn by an interest in the fine arts—acting, set decoration and architecture—and groping for a creative life while stuck in the study of physical existence. Jenny Thurman's cooking kept me well fed, the paychecks were good, and I figured there was plenty of—well, that's enough, more than enough, about me. Let me take us back to the day that the sun lined up after the wind swept over the ridge and changed the young couple's lives.

Mrs. Thurman had been whistling in the kitchen while making dinner, waddling to and from the oven to check on the pot roast while chopping celery she had picked in the vegetable garden and washed in the sink. She was six months pregnant, happy as can be and glowing with joy and she got around just fine. I remember the day like it was ten seconds ago; the smell of the roast in the oven, the melody of Mrs. Thurman's tune, looping up, down and around with gaiety, even the sight of the bright red rosebushes and yellow and green lemon trees on the sloping yard just outside Dr. Thurman's study. He had his face buried in a book as usual, sighing as his pale young wife shuffled and whistled a few steps away, with a corner of his mouth almost smiling. The touchy master looked as close to happy as I'd seen him, like a young Jimmy Stewart always bothered by something but sort of comfortable in his irritation.

Mrs. Thurman had decided to get out of the heat in the kitchen and, after pouring herself a glass of iced lemonade, took the beverage and a new biography to the outdoor patio to rest, relax and enjoy the warm winds. The pot roast would take a while to cook anyway.

Then it came. That horrid sound: the sound of a civil defense siren. The sound of it pierced the house, the ranch, the valley—as if time abruptly stood still and the three of us fell into a nightmare, unable to move, scream or look away. I shall remember the look on Dr. Thurman's face as his eyes widened and he stood and moved toward the plate glass window overlooking his sprawling ranch in the San Fernando Valley. I could see that he was hearing the alarm and scouting the scene. I would later learn that an unseen cloud was creeping over the ridge. He looked puzzled. He looked paralyzed.

My own mind raced—I'd lived in Europe during the war—and I was transfixed by the physics professor. Were we under attack? I wondered. The Soviets had been making threats. Communist China had crossed into Korea. MacArthur had been fired. Pearl Harbor had been bombed not that long ago. Was this some sort of earthquake alert? Or was it something else? When the magnitude of what might be happening struck me, the steno pad I'd been using for dictation tumbled from my lap. I took notice of the time on the clock on Dr. Thurman's desk. It was a quarter past one o'clock in the afternoon. Jenny Thurman, as unaware as we were that a radioactive cloud was coming our way, had looked up, put the book down and slowly turned to scan the landscape to see if she could see anything happening. A white curtain in the kitchen danced in the breeze.

With square-jawed Theodore Thurman searching the

valley through the plate-glass window in the study and Mrs. Thurman oblivious to what was going on, facing and inhaling the valley's air, I was held by the prospect of something horrible happening. Maybe it was the memory of war but something dreadful rose from within me. Sharp sirens rang in a continuous loop, punctuated by brief pauses of heart-stopping silence. I could see Jenny Thurman's round-bellied figure and caught glimpses of her chestnut-brown hair blowing in the breeze from where I sat in the study and, a few feet away, I saw the back and profile of Dr. Thurman with a puzzled expression, which was mixed with consternation. My heart pounded, my temples pulsated, and I felt a kind of terror seep into my soul. In an instant, I was blinded by a powerful bolt of light. The sun had changed position. It had begun to set.

I remember thinking, as the sunlight slipped over the horizon, was that I wished I had become an artist instead.

At that moment, the siren stopped. Dr. Thurman stood motionless. Mrs. Thurman was immobile on the patio. I heard only the sound of the curtain at the kitchen window whipping in the wind. We would soon learn through news reports that we had been enshrouded in a radioactive cloud. I must have muttered some sort of inquiry to Dr. Thurman during the incident, because he replied about not having enough time, and I reacted by flying from room to room around the house shuttering as many windows as I could, though not without first gently moving Mrs. Thurman inside and to a corner of the breakfast booth. I had no clue what had happened, but I spent the rest of the evening going back to the guest house and the barn to check windows and livestock and taking precautionary measures on the pre-supposition that the air might be harmful. In the days and weeks ahead, Theodore and Jenny Thurman were beside themselves; Dr. Thurman was perturbed, and Mrs. Thurman was dazed. Thus began an unusual journey in time.

My name is Mabus.

This is not my story—this is his. It is the tale of a man who sought to set things right—and quite decisively—or is it quite possibly?—did.

Chapter 2: Newborn

Mrs. Thurman went into labor a few months later. She named the newborn Jeff, short for the American president she had admired as a history major in college. There was much more that happened during that childbirth. But, first, about that cloud.

There had been an incident at the nuclear lab nestled in the foothills of Los Angeles, not far from the Thurman ranch. Following a malfunction, the nuclear reactor had apparently continued to operate, though radiation had already been released into the atmosphere. The incident did not result in a meltdown, at least not a meltdown in the strictest sense. Or at least that is what we were led to believe.

The facility, known as Rocketdyne and the Santa Susana Field Laboratory, is a positive memory because the lab was the lifeblood of the San Fernando, Simi and Conejo valleys, employing thousands and fueling the hopes, goals and lives of everyone who sought to realize that distinctively early 1960s' southern California dream. That it might have become a nightmare at the nuclear lab—where the accident occurred—is another issue. Santa Susana was a blessing for what it represented.

We once drove up at night, under a black sky, and we came upon the place bathed in manmade lights shining like a bejeweled crown, sitting atop sandstone and granite outcroppings. Lights, towers, gantries and buildings struck me with awe as an earthbound gateway to Heaven.

Winding further up mountain roads, you could pull over in plain sight of lab workers mounting rocket engines one by one on test stands overhanging small canyons. Using what Dr. Thurman had explained was every type of fuel known to man, they fired up the engines. My eyes widened when Santa Susana bellowed and belched with roaring fire and white smoke, rumbling and shaking as engineers test-fired engines, with over a million pounds of thrust bursting from a single source. Sitting in the car with Dr. Thurman, every engine felt as if a volcano was erupting beneath us. I was entranced.

Most nearby houses, including the Thurman ranch house, had single-pane windows, which would shake until the fuel was exhausted, which would later amuse the Dr. and Mrs. Thurman's friends and new neighbors experiencing it during their first visit. He would usually explain that Santa Susana was our neighborhood volcano. Workers pumped thousands of gallons of water into the exhaust to cool the belching fire and dampen the sound, but it was too much to contain.

Santa Susana was the power source where they built engines and tested them for everything from powering supersonic x-planes to propelling astronauts into space for Apollo moon landings. What I didn't know, what we did not know, was that it was also the source of Jeff Thurman's yet to be discovered ability to sense what was about to happen, in his visions and nightmares. It was a source of emerging and mysterious science which would be kept hidden from the public for 20 years. The bustling, exciting and cryptic work at Santa Susana would become the catalyst for the child Jeff's bold and imaginative vision of the future.

Just a mile away to the North, on the other side of "The Hill", as it became known among locals, was a new, spreading counterculture—a drug subculture—which would bleed out the old, Golden Age of Hollywood and make way for a new, stained way of living that really had very little to do with living at all. Beyond this futuristic mountain, where man set about making and realizing exciting and positive goals for next generations, where silent movies were once made featuring Roy Rogers, Dale Evans, Monty Montana and real cowboys and movie stars, the hippies had started taking up residence at a place called Spahn Ranch. They burrowed in caves in and around the Santa Susana Knowles, a small, rocky landscape where the lowest losers met, tempted and coaxed the most vulnerable waifs, misfits and street urchins to cast about evil under the sight and sound and rumble of that enthralling rocket mountain. The dark ranch was the flipside of the Santa Susana science lab. The lab represented life; the hippie compound on the other side of the mountain represented the anti-life. Each would climax in two separate, opposite events in the year 1969—Apollo moon landing and Manson Family mass murder—and both would be distantly relevant to the essence of our tale in time.

But for now, we turn back to the speculation among scientists about the cause of that nuclear accident, speculation which lasted for months. Newspapers covered the story, and the mystery of the small radiation leak and its origins wound up in a few lonely sentences buried deep within the newspaper. There were no apparent signs of major after-effects from the radiation. The growing San Fernando Valley communities, bursting with a new middle class, were unfazed. The 1959 nuclear incident came to be known as an anomaly. Probably related to faulty procedures, some said.

Logs were checked and re-checked. A government commission was formed. A report was filed. The consensus seemed to be that the lab needed more controls, but no one had identified the cause.

Mrs. Thurman was in her eighth month of pregnancy when one day she went into labor around midnight. After being admitted to the Hospital she started hemorrhaging. Her labor was long and arduous, and, at some point, it dawned on her doctors that both mother and child could not survive. Either her life would expire or the fetus would have to be terminated. The mother was losing blood—she was losing it fast—and the fetus was viable; the mother, it was explained to her husband , was not. Jenny Thurman bled to death while giving birth. She was pronounced dead by her obstetrician at eight minutes past the hour. The child named for Thomas Jefferson was kept alive.

Dr. Thurman was devastated.

He drove home from the hospital in a fog. His wife's body was in the morgue. His newborn son was in chronic danger. And Theodore Thurman pulled up to his ranch house, turned off the ignition and headlights and sat alone in the carport for a period of three hours.

I'd been dealing all day with phone calls from relatives, reading over laboratory reports, tending to the needs of the Thurman household, including an especially demanding hired hand I'd recently brought on named Harriet, who required constant supervision. The portly woman had been hired to do light housekeeping and she was already rearranging furniture. Just when I'd set her back to washing and vacuuming, there she was redecorating and redesigning. I finally told her to take time for lunch and make herself a sandwich. She couldn't do that right, either. She made a plate of sandwiches for the ranch hands and household staff. I have to say they were the best I'd ever had.

And I was ready for a break. At dusk, as the sun descended into that particular spot in the office that made it impossible to get anything done, I stepped outside for a spell.

I noticed the doctor immediately: a tall, solid frame slumped over the steering wheel. I could see that it was him. I rushed over and leveraged his body weight with my hands to help him out of the car, limb by limb. He felt limp and heavy, slouching shoulders, slow-moving eyelids and a mouth that did not move. When he looked up, his eyes were empty. His face was contorted in puzzlement, shock and despair.

I never saw him smile again.

From that moment on, Dr. Theodore Thurman was smaller to me than he had been. He would complain about the mailman being late. He would snarl when I arrived for work at dawn and greet him with 'good morning'. He'd groan when I bid 'good evening' before leaving the office. Finally, he insisted that I move into a guest room and start helping around the house, so he didn't have to put up with me coming and going. His work was important, yet his life had come undone. My help was essential, or so it was implied.

I'd been renting a studio apartment above a nightclub on Sunset Boulevard in Hollywood since I'd come to Los Angeles. As many did, I came to Hollywood for a motion picture production job, which in my case I had heard about from the director of a Bavarian dance troupe. The job as a set designer had ended long ago and I'd been struggling. I'd worked in MGM's wardrobe department, waited tables at a French bistro and danced with elderly guests at the Ambassador Hotel every Saturday night. Dr. Thurman's job, which came as a referral through an acquaintance whose mother was a clerical worker at Cal Tech, had been a steady income, for which I was very grateful. My small apartment needed a new coat of paint and a kitchen, so when Dr. Thurman indicated his preference, I did not hesitate to move. I cleared and stored Mrs. Thurman's things, did this and that around the ranch, balancing books and serving as his assistant, and I tried to keep Harriet out of Dr. Thurman's way. I practically ran the place.

Dr. Thurman was an ornery employer. He'd complain about the weather—too hot, too cold, too much the same—about the music coming from the ice cream truck, youngsters playing in the street, which they did back then, or the rock music blaring from a passing car radio. Worst of all, he'd snap at the sound of his son's laughter. It was as if joy had been banished from his home and life. Slowly and steadily, Dr. Thurman lost any real connection to his values. When Jenny Thurman died, so did his spirit.

It was I who wound up caring for Jeff when the child came home from the hospital. Sadly, Dr. Thurman had no tolerance for his child. The scientist plunged into his work, refusing to tend to the boy's needs, or, for that matter, to his own. He wouldn't eat. He couldn't sleep. He was like an exposed nerve ending, obsessing over stacks of papers and books, making meticulous notes and measurements on various physics theories. At night, he'd wander the grounds, sitting in the darkness on the terrace behind the house staring up at the stars.

As the assistant during those years, I would step into his study in silence, careful to move deftly around the strategically placed piles of paper, setting down one of Harriet's sandwiches (which he wouldn't eat) within his peripheral vision, or sitting at my corner desk in the sunken part of his office for hours grading papers, paying bills, or deciphering notes and tabulations. We worked in a tense, stifling isolation. Other than an occasional lecture or scholarly conference at Cal Tech, we rarely went out. We barely spoke. We worked each day until sundown.

Being a caretaker to Jeff and a secretary to Dr. Thurman was a lot to bear. With the tacit consent of Dr. Thurman, and against my better judgment, I promoted Harriet to head housekeeper and nanny so she could help out with Jeff. The rotund woman gave me no end of grief with her constantly cheerful personality and deviations from her work schedule, but we did share cleaning duties and she helped me to make the meals and care for the infant, then toddler, who grew into a rambunctious boy. Eventually, Harriet's background in accounting helped immensely with the Thurman ranch's voluminous bookkeeping. Harriet also agreed to take up whatever chores I deemed necessary at a moment's notice. She was incorrigible—and she was admittedly indispensable.

At each day's sunset, the bony, unhappy doctor would pull himself up and rise from a creaky wooden chair, arch his back with his hands on the posterior of his hips, groan or grumble and exit the room in a snort or a tromp. He took the joy out of any activity, from sharpening a pencil—he'd bark that the grinding was making too much noise—to correcting an erroneous calculation, which he'd insist had been born of my constant distraction or the sound of his son buzzing while playing with a toy airplane in the backyard. Theodore Thurman was forty-one years old.

In his time—and Jenny's widower was not alive for long after she died—the measurements, experiments and conclusions were constructive, but they seemed to proceed with neither purpose nor relevance. His work was increasingly displayed in countless stacks of single sheets of paper, yellowing writing tablets, scribbled graphs, notations and books scattered throughout the office. He had been ornery before Jeff was born, but he had been known to laugh, and he at least occasionally had enjoyed the company of his wife Jenny, whose bookish happiness at small and ordinary occurrences he seemed to prize in his own way. When she died, Dr. Thurman hated the world.

Each evening after Dr. Thurman retired, as I tidied up, collecting coffee cups and fresh vegetable platters and placing the dishes onto empty trays, retrieving crumpled papers and cigarette butts that hadn't made it to the trashcan or ashtray, our incubator of an office was suddenly still, as if paused for a respite from his bitter and miserable presence.

At each sundown, Dr. Thurman's office would briefly become surrounded by the Santa Susana mountains, which would appear to take on new, taller dimensions in the shadows caused by the shifting sun, trembling for a few moments, plainly framed by the large picture window made of beveled glass. Each day at that time, in a dazzling display caused by certain angles and juxtapositions of glass, metal and ranch house architecture, sunlight would consume the place so completely that nothing could be done—work was impossible—and time stood still. Every sunset was a source of golden light infused into another gray, dreary day, as though the sun was daring us into the future.

The future for Dr. Thurman was not to be.

Chapter 3: Jeff

Theodore Thurman died on a Monday morning.

I woke up, went about my business making coffee in the percolator, looking over the feed supply, crop conditions and other ranch business, getting Jeff ready for pre-school, and making my rounds on the ranch before heading into the office down the hall. I found Dr. Thurman slumped over his desk.

"Good morning, Sir." I'd greeted dispassionately, bending over his desk to check the daily schedule. He did not answer.

We had played this game for years. I greeted Dr. Thurman each morning. He typically mumbled or ignored me—it was not unusual to find him asleep at his desk—and we went about our studies, calculations and note making. On other days, we'd conduct experiments—those were my favorite workdays—or test equipment.

This time, he did not stir. I could sometimes detect at least a moan for coffee—and, as I looked again, I could see that he was the color of early morning frost. Cold to the touch. I felt a stab of shock, which was momentary, because I can't honestly say I was surprised. I took a breath to brace for this reality and I reached for the telephone to call an ambulance. Dr. Thurman was pronounced dead on arrival at the same hospital where his wife had died three and a half years earlier. Jeff's parents were gone.

I still don't know the cause of death. As I stood in the entrance hall and announced the news to the ranch hands and household staff, the thought occurred to me that he had died of a ruptured soul, which is not exactly a broken heart. The help were shocked, but not saddened, and, as executor and Jeff's guardian, I let some of the non-essential employees go and, knowing that their burdens would increase given the new context, gave Harriet and Ned the groundskeeper a pay raise. The will had been read, the estate had been settled, and I was to inherit everything until Jeff reached the age of consent. I was set for life. Suddenly, too, I was a bachelor parent—and I found that Jefferson Thurman was an extraordinary child.

During his hospitalization while a premature infant, Jeff had been acutely aware of anyone's presence, including ours during my visits with Dr. Thurman, even before we would reach his bassinet. My visits had been more attentive as we instantly bonded over a stuffed tiger I'd purchased at the gift shop and nicknamed Tugs (because Jeff kept pulling at the stuffed animal).

Curiously, as soon as we'd come within a few feet of his bassinet, he'd stop stirring or making noises, and he seemed to extend his tiny pink arms for a grab at Tugs. Once within range, he didn't wriggle, he didn't cry, he didn't fuss—not like other premature infants in the ward. He was an astute observer, as cautious as he was curious.

The nurses and doctors were fascinated by this particular patient. They'd monitor Jeff's vital signs, and whisper about his remarkable progress. Upon each visit, a band of doctors and nurses greeted us with stories of eager feedings and updates on his condition.

"How's the heart rate?" Dr. Thurman would declare more than he would ask, avoiding reference to his son as a person, let alone referring to Jeff by name.

Once engaged, hospital staff would try to involve Dr. Thurman in his child's medical treatment.

"Mmm-hmm, mmm-hmm. His breathing? OK. Motor skills? Alright. What about his brain functions?"

Dr. Thurman had had a commanding presence. His eyes were an almost translucent gray and his closely cropped haircut gave him a military look that, topping a six-foot frame, made an impression. When he bent down to inspect the tiny body that was his son, Jeff's blue-gray eyes stared up at him and held his gaze.

I admit I sort of took to the child. Whenever I could see that Jeff was about to erupt into some unpleasant expression—usually when he let out a gasp—"Gah!"—I tried to move into his sight line.

Mirroring the infant's concerned facial map, I stood over him and made sure he saw me. Little Jeff focused on my long, rubbery face long enough to relax and we eased into a game with Tugs the tiger, whose tail I wagged with my index finger, much to the boy's delight. I don't remember what ridiculous sounds I made, I know only that I made them and it seemed to work. Jeff Thurman was entranced. Once while witnessing this interplay, Dr. Thurman had stepped back, examining the exchange. Noting Jeff's resemblance to his late mother, Jenny, he added, gravely but evenly: "If he makes it out of here, I want you to take care of him."

I was no longer shocked by what he said or did. The man was still mired in grief.

"What about your family?" I asked.

"No" came the reply as he turned and exited the ward while the nurse took Jeff's chart and made some notes.

That was that. There were to be no more Mrs. Thurman, no more children, and no more caregiving. His pronouncement had signaled an end to the promise of happiness for the tall, reedy physicist, father and widower; he had disconnected from the world, and he was having none of this creature beneath us. I was Jeff's surrogate parent.

It was a role I initially did not relish, feeling further distanced from finishing work as Dr. Thurman's assistant and pursuing my own goals, but his father had alienated Jeff with such heartbreaking finality that I felt compelled to provide basic parenting. I thought about Harriet, who had visited Jeff in the ward a few times and assumed the role of Jeff's nanny. But I also knew that Harriet was not cut out for the rigors of motherhood.

When Dr. Thurman died, leaving his papers, studies and estate to Jeff in care of me, who would raise him, I knew I would do my best.

I asked Harriet to work extra hours and I also gave her the red and white 1958 Ford Fairlane Skyliner that Mrs. Thurman had used, which was enough to keep her happy. I made sure Jeff had the best of everything— fresh meat, poultry and eggs from the ranch and local farms—and I sent him to pre-school. Later, I enrolled Jeff in a private academy that emphasized science, history and English. I cooked, fed and dressed him each morning, drove him to school, and let him play with neighbor children after school after checking his homework. I read adventure stories and tucked him in every night. He slept with Tugs at his side. Sometimes, Harriet would set Tugs on the dresser and forget to restore the stuffed animal to the bed. "Tuggy Tiger," Jeff would say at bedtime. It was more of a demand than a request.

As the child grew older, I cooked, assigned chores and attended parent-teacher conferences. We had dinner every evening at sundown. When prompted, he'd talk about baseball, history and outer space, whatever he wished to talk about, really. I rarely moved the conversation. For one thing, I was too exhausted by sundown and Harriet, who would serve dinner and sit with us yammering about whatever she was reading, barely let me get a word out of my mouth. But those evenings were fine. There was a silent code and we all knew I was in charge of the child until such time as the child took charge of his life. I was a guardian in the true sense—a parent in the fundamental sense—with the ghost of Jenny Thurman as the absent custodian of our busy, hardworking family life. Jeff was a bright, quiet child—proficient in sports, excellent in school and insatiably curious about the world.

He desperately wanted a mother. Not that Harriet wasn't a fine woman of strong character and a decent nanny. But having her look after the boy wasn't the same as having a mother.

"Mabus?" he asked one morning over pancakes. "What was my mom like?"

I knew from my own studies in child psychology that the question was coming. Strange as it may sound for a middle-aged bachelor, and former artist, living on a ranch in the early 1960s, I had delved into the science of raising a child. I dared not miss a beat when the six-year-old launched his inquisition.

"Oh, she was warm and lovely," I replied, setting maple syrup on the Formica breakfast table and looking him square in the eye.

It was true. I told him what I remembered about Jenny Thurman.

"Your mother had a strong sense of right and wrong, Jeff," I said, glancing sideways at the boy while buttering some toast. "I know that she was very interested in the world. She liked to read and cook, and she enjoyed learning about new ideas. She would go into the library and sit down and read book after book."

"What did she read about?" Her son wanted to know.

"Oh, she'd read about Ancient Greece, early Americans and Western pioneers," I answered, pausing to look out at the ranch and remember her walking along its paths. "She would talk about what she'd read and learned for days. She knew a lot about Greeks, Founding Fathers, and cowboys. She wanted to share her interest with you." I looked over and saw Harriet napping on the living room sofa. "Your mother had beautiful brown eyes," I told him, "And every time I looked at her she seemed to be laughing inside. She was full of joy."

He looked at me and his eyes, which resembled his mother's, widened. "She twinkled every time she talked about you," I told Jeff. "She was never happier than when she was expecting you."

He looked down at his plate for a moment at the thought. "What I meant what was…what was my mom like before she had me," he said, looking up and into my eyes. "Before my father".

"Well, I didn't know your mother then," I explained. I said I did remember one time shortly after they were married and I'd been hired.

"Your father was studying at Cal Tech one day and your mother and I were alone for an afternoon. We went out and sat on the back porch drinking lemonade, looking over the ranch and out at the hills, talking about her childhood." Jeff stopped eating and leaned forward, aroused by the answer. "Yes?"

"Well," I continued, "she said that she had been raised here in the Valley and had loved working in her family's orange groves, picking oranges off the trees all day. She liked getting dirty like her brothers, but she had also longed to go off to college to get an education about things that matter in life."

"Why?" He wanted to know. It was his favorite question. You could count on him asking it at least 11 times a day.

"Because, she said she knew that there was evil in the world, and she knew that there was good, and she knew it wasn't always easy to tell the difference, but she wanted very much to find out why. She figured that college was where people went to learn such things." My back porch conversation with Mrs. Thurman, a rare occurrence resulting from a patch of downtime due to Dr. Thurman's delay, had been a pleasure. I'd forgotten how much I had enjoyed it. Her words had given me a new, deeper respect for Jenny Thurman. She was one of the reasons I had stayed on.

I told Jeff that she had remembered her grandfather bursting out of the house, running into the groves, calling out that the Japanese had attacked Pearl Harbor. She recalled the fear of being invaded, and the horror of the Nazis and the Soviets. She said that after the war everyone thought everything was fine—but she said that, even as a girl, she didn't think everything was fine. In fact, not unlike Jeff, she didn't understand why everyone else did.

I told him that and it seemed to satisfy something inside him. He sat for a while, looking out the breakfast nook window at the winding road that led down into the San Fernando Valley. Finally, he said, to himself, "that's interesting." At that, I stood and gathered the breakfast dishes. We were quiet for a few moments. I washed the dishes, reminding Jeff that it was time to get ready for school, and we both listened to the sound of Harriet snoring. He asked, "So, did my mother go to college?"

"Yes, she did," I replied. "She studied and earned good grades. And, graduated with honors. She majored in history."

"I wish she knew me," he said looking out the window again.

"Time for school, Jeff," I said firmly. "I don't want you to be late for attendance." I had decided early in my child development research not to yield to his idle speculation. I'd wanted to say, "So do I." I think he knew it.

Jeff was not a model student. He was exceptionally intelligent, prone to questions, providing slow, thoughtful answers, and he routinely wore down his erasers. Even his best teachers couldn't keep up and there weren't many of those despite the academy's vaunted curriculum. His penmanship was atrocious, his spelling was a challenge, and he had a slight speech impediment until he was seven years old. Jeff was an awkward boy, with a haircut that was out of fashion, an overbite from his father's side and athletic skills hampered by a habit of punching the school bully whenever a fellow student was targeted—which perpetually got him bumped from the starting roster. Jeff wound up in the headmaster's office more than a few times. He never made varsity teams for this reason.

One night in January 1971, something else happened. Jeff awakened from a nightmare about the earth shaking and buildings collapsing. He woke up with a yelp—I heard Harriet running down the hall to Jeff's room—and told me at breakfast that he had a terrible headache. When a major earthquake rocked Los Angeles a few weeks later, we all thought it was a coincidence.

Years went by. Puberty came at the age of fifteen. The voice creaked, the pores clogged, and the hair grew more unruly and greasy—and he shut himself away more than usual as he discovered the emerging functions of his body. It was difficult for Jeff to handle puberty as well as having disturbing dreams and debilitating headaches, which doctors were unable to diagnose, but he carried on.

Jeff graduated from the academy largely unspoiled by the cultural turmoil of the 1960s and 1970s. He didn't take southern California's hippies and their slogans seriously and he grew into a handsome young rancher who knew how to milk a cow, load, handle and fire a gun responsibly, and Jeff loved his country and had a mind of his own. When he came across draft dodgers, rabble-rousers and drug pushers on college campuses while researching college admissions, he was more amused than alarmed.

Jeff knew that he had been sheltered, and he knew this meant he would probably be resented in college, but he possessed an enthusiasm for life that combined his mother's buoyancy with his father's drive. Afflicted with headaches and plagued by sporadic nightmares—he'd reported that the latest episode was about an abused child—Jeff had become fascinated by his father's writings about physics, life and time. Besides a college education, he wanted to work in a laboratory, do research and study new theories. Jeff, like Jenny Thurman, wanted to learn.

He attended and graduated college with a degree in physics, and, by 1990, he had worked and experimented in the best national labs. When he drove up the road to the ranch, stepped out of the pickup truck he'd bought used, and returned home to attend graduate school at CalTech, Jeff was a man—with his father's drive, his mother's decency, and, I say this modestly, with not in small measure my diligence.

He didn't know it then, the formerly awkward kid with a stuffed tiger named Tugs, but Jeff Thurman would need them all very much.

Chapter 4: Nightmare

Thrashing about in bed, Jeff's body jerked.

"No!" he called out in a voice, which sounded part man, part beast. "Stop!"

Swirling in another nightmare, Jeff's latest series of dreams took a darker turn. This nightmare was about a child being abused.

Until now, he'd been hearing a child's screams. He had dreamt of running toward a locked door, jiggling a jammed, brass doorknob only to be blasted backward by a huge, unstoppable force.

However, in this dream, he turned the knob and the door opened. What he saw was unspeakable: a girl—an older man—foreign objects—the use of force—a trickle of blood—rape. She was struggling. She was losing. Jeff didn't know who she was—nor was he able to make out an image of the man hurting her—but he knew he had to stop it.

Jeff ran toward the man, whose back faced him, to pull him off the girl. As he charged toward them, Jeff felt a revulsion he'd never felt before, like something had crawled up inside of his stomach and died, and it was having convulsions. The chocolate brown-haired girl was staring at him, her hazel eyes glazed like no child's eyes should be. She finally closed her eyes, as if his effort was futile, and drifted away. Jeff felt his body spasm and jerk. He woke up in a fit.

"Nooo!!!" It was guttural scream.

Portly Harriet lurched from her bed toward Jeff's room. When Jeff went to college, I had her stay on at the ranch as my assistant, and since he'd returned to attend Cal Tech, she had tended to Jeff during his nightmares. He slept in his old room, which I had remodeled. That night, I leapt to my feet, too, and met Harriet in the doorway.

This time, I shooed her away; it was my turn.

I entered the room and stood over him, jostling his shoulder. "What is it, Jeff?" I asked, setting a bath towel at his side. "Another earthquake? Assassination? The helpless child?"

"A kid," he answered in a growl, propping up on his elbows. "The girl. She's—she's being assaulted," Jeff looked up at me with a combination of disgust and the look of a plea. He was dripping in sweat. His voice was low. "I tried to stop it."

I looked at him. "Anyone you know?" I asked, reaching for the bathrobe hanging on the back of his bedroom door and handing it to him as he toweled himself off.

"No," he said, exhausted. "I've asked a top psychologist, I've talked to the psych experts at school, and I've read about this type of recurring nightmare. I haven't figured it out. I don't fit the profile for someone usually plagued by such nightmares – I haven't been traumatized – and I haven't been diagnosed with post-traumatic stress disorder." His voice was detached, not dejected. He ran his fingers through his chestnut-colored hair, pulled himself together, paused, stood up and put the robe on. I handed him a glass of water—he drank it up. "I want to know what's causing them," he finally said.

The night sky cast a dark blue glow over the ranch and into the bedroom, which still bore some marks of decoration in the astronomy theme we'd selected when Jeff was eight years old. Faded, twinkling stars on the wallpaper, planets on the ceiling. Only now there was a full-sized dresser, bedroom furniture and a telescope by the sliding glass door.

Jeff the adult was neither gangly nor awkward—he was loose-limbed yet stiff and tense in posture and manner, making you feel at ease yet formal at once. He lumbered into the kitchen, opened the refrigerator and grabbed a bottle of cold beer.

"It was the most frustrating one I've had," he said in a whisper, not wanting to disturb Harriet, who had gone back to her room. "She stares straight through me, like she's a ghost and there's nothing I can do," he said, taking a gulp and swallowing it down. "I'm helpless, Mabus." He looked at the floor. "I feel awful."

"Do you know her?" I asked.

"No," Jeff replied, shaking his head, searching his mind.

"Who do you know that's in trouble?" I asked, using my limited knowledge of dream theories.

"There's Gina, who works in the lab at school. Her mother is always on her about something. But she's 31 and, besides, she is not the helpless type. My friend Alan from Oxford wrote last week that his grandfather had died in London, and he said he was feeling blue. That's about it." He said, leaning against the counter. "I'm concerned that it's another of my mother issues."

I nodded, knowing that he had his fair share of those.

"The best thing to do is wait and see if this happens again," I said. "If it's recurring, it may be related to the loss of your parents, linked to abandonment trauma."

"Mabus, what if the dreams are real? What if they are premonitions of things to come, or happening right now? Even if I know who these people are, and could do something about them, protect them somehow, at what point do you know the proper course of action?

I said, "Well, I don't know. I suppose I don't know about premonitions. Good Samaritans help others in trouble if they can. Heroes risk their lives. Then there are vigilantes and there are avengers and there's a difference. Then there are murderers. The definitions and labels vary from situation to situation, culture to culture. If it is possible that the nightmares are some type of appearance or glimpse of reality, you'd better decide which one you are."

Jeff concurred with a nod and finished the beer, placing the bottle in the trash.

"Good night, Mabus," he said, half-smiling, like a jock who's about the re-enter the ring to his coach. "See you in the morning."

"Goodnight, Jeff."

The next few nights were uneventful. The days, too. We worked on the ranch in the mornings, while Harriet brewed weak coffee and burned the toast before waddling over to the office to keep the books. Jeff would take over the dining room table with textbooks, shuttling to Cal Tech for classes, coming home to stay up all night writing papers and studying for exams. It was good to have him home.

Over the years, I had managed the ranch, making a hobby of my work in the arts, and I had recently managed to finish some old drawings in my makeshift studio out in the barn. I had even sold a still life painting during a gallery showing in Brentwood. Aside from her sandwiches, Harriet was a terrible cook, a mediocre assistant, and a marvel at bookkeeping. As an operational ranch, we'd have been lost without her. Everyone was terribly busy.

Through hard work, the Thurman ranch was profitable. Harriet was an expert administrator, managing workers, schedule, and payroll, and I ran the place, studying soil conditions, fruits and vegetables, and handling major transactions. The business balanced my artistic pursuits, which were less predictable than vegetable crops, and we enjoyed our work. Jeff would do quite well when the property's value was assessed should something happen to us. He had inherited the ranch when he turned 21, kept us on, and let us run the place. He checked the books once a year at Christmastime. He never said a word other than "good job," and besides an annual Christmas bonus and the best Christmas office party in the San Fernando Valley—at a club overlooking the Sepulveda Pass—that was that.

But I was getting too old to be in the studio for hours at a time and couldn't stand to be in the fields for more than an hour. We both knew that he would eventually take over the ranch when he finished grad school and make a lot more money with a lot less effort.

Jeff could examine soil, calculate figures, and size up an operation's efficiency, increasing productivity and profits in what amounted to a few minutes. That he did it on a break between physics class and advanced calculus left everyone in amazement. Jeff had surpassed his father in ability and he knew it. He was a genius.

Unlike Dr. Thurman, Jeff was also a man of the world, delighting in the happiness of those he cared about, from the newest hired ranch hand to this crumbling old artist. Every fall, he'd take the ranchers' kids on a hayride, and on the weekends the three of us would go to the movies. My favorite memories were the numerous daytime excursions and evenings at the symphony, the ballet or jazz concerts at the Hollywood Bowl. I was coming to the final years of my life and I took particular pleasure in being able to share great works of art with Jeff as we approached the 21st century at last. It was like seeing him off into a better, brighter future. I think Jenny Thurman would have liked that.

We sampled works by Chopin, Mozart and Brahms at concert halls throughout California. We toured antiquities, towering sculptures and magnificent busts, paintings by the Impressionists, meticulous Japanese gardens and astonishing documents, films, and artifacts at the Huntington, the Getty and old movie theaters. We took in Art Deco and modern architecture on the avenues and hills of Los Angeles at places built by Richard Neutra, John Lautner, and Frank Lloyd Wright, and the Griffith Park Observatory. Jeff, who had studied and interned across the world in London, Switzerland, and Hong Kong, was emboldened by each field trip.

"The wonder of man," he'd observed after attending one concert in downtown Los Angeles. He drove us home exalted, spilling himself into a recreation of the composer's crescendo while taking on the Hollywood freeway, laughing all the way, and describing the concert in glorious detail to artistically challenged Harriet, her hair in curlers while trying to watch television, once we walked in the door. She wound up entranced just the same, a curler dangling in front of her face as she giggled with delight.

When I noticed an item in the paper that the Tantham Ballet was coming to town, I knew we had to attend. If I'd taught him nothing, I'd taught Jeff the importance of acting on one's values, and seeing dancers spring to soaring music was one of mine. I wasn't going to miss experiencing it with Jeff. It was fine for Harriet to sit and watch the latest television episode or read her mundane mystery novels, but life was a feast and Jeff would relish pulling up a chair.

He had one night free from his studies and his dating—he had been meeting young women with whom he had connected on the Internet at various cafes—and that was the night the Tantham Ballet was scheduled to perform at the City Concert Hall. I had bought the tickets weeks in advance and obtained front row-center seats. We wouldn't miss a thing.

Jeff rushed home from school, tossed the car keys on the kitchen table, and tore into the house to change into his formalwear. He had grown into an attractive young man, no longer the gawky teenager at prom or graduation, or the eager and petulant young college graduate of a few years ago. Tonight, he was a dashing gentleman.

Jeff had met and dated a variety of women, some overly intellectual—fellow scientists with something to prove—some too shallow, and none just perfect. After each breakup or disappointment, he'd made his way home, or written in letters or e-mail, expressing his deep and closely held loneliness. There, in the silence of being an only child raised by a nanny and an assistant, he was always yearning for the perfect partner in his quest for happiness.

Whenever Jeff had experienced a moment of joy from one of his achievements, whether an award-winning science project or an honorable distinction, it was followed by a tinge of sadness that he had no equal with whom to share his triumph, a feeling rooted in the loss of his mother.

"How was your date?" I had asked one night when he came in during those first weeks home for grad school.

He had paused wearily at the front door, slowly closing it, listening to it catch. He moved in slow motion, as if reluctant to turn around and face the question. "Mabus?" he asked and answered, seeming younger than his 34 years, "do you think true love is possible?"

I watched his anguish from my perch in the living room, a rather grand old, weathered chair with a stand-alone reading lamp at its side.

I reflected on Jeff's question.

"Of course it is," I said. "I have seen it. I haven't felt it."

He turned around.

"So, how do you know?" He asked.

"Because your mother felt that way about your father, and vice versa. At least in the beginning," I added, which was true.

"I want more than that," he said with no trace of anger, having figured that fact out by himself. "I want to be loved, Mabus, for the best of me, and I want a woman who's not threatened by it."

I put my book down at that, slightly impressed that he had figured that out, too. "That won't be easy," I explained. "The world is full of women who hate men, men who seek that in a woman—and women who seek exactly that in a man."

"Why?" He said, reverting to his favorite question.

"Because we live in an age of envy," I answered. "Listen to what Chopin composed, read what Ibsen wrote, look at what Houdon made with his hands—what Galileo saw in the stars—see how they are regarded today. Look at what men do to man."

"Why?" He asked again, this time stepping forward and looking angry.

"Man is taught to deny himself, or to act as though he does," I said. "Almost everyone believes that it's acceptable to denigrate man." I looked at him sternly, never feeling more like his father than I did in that moment, and I leaned forward and told him: "Only it isn't, so don't. And don't go near the woman who does." I'd never heard myself sound like that before—a kind of low, commanding tone I didn't think I had in me.

Jeff smiled. It was a knowing, benevolent grin, easy and familiar. The life had come back to his eyes. He didn't say anything; he just walked over toward the chair, stood next to the reading lamp, bent down and kissed my forehead.

That was then, and here he was a few years later dressing for the ballet.

"It's show time, Mabus," he said, emerging from his room and pointing to his wristwatch while I fiddled with a cuff link.

At the ballet, Jeff was instantly drawn to one of the principal dancers. She was not the lead ballerina, but she stood out from the others. Her movements were more extended and her leaps were elongated, as though she lingered a moment and hovered on a certain feat, point or musical note. Her arms were like tree branches on a night when the wind brushes against the treetops, when everything undulates and moves with a kind of rhythm. The pirouettes were perfect, with her hand bent slightly above her arm in an arc, and she danced like an arrow aiming in our direction. She was radiant.

Jeff noticed. He sat and watched, applauded at each interval, and when the final curtain fell and the company took their bows, he stared at her with an intensity of desire I had never seen in his eyes. I understood it immediately—she was like the physical form of his spirit; a union of ideals, equations, and desires in a single unit that was a woman's body. After the final bow, with floral arrangements lining the edge of the stage, he turned to me, said he'd meet me by the marquee, and excused himself. He would find his way backstage, where he would meet a shy ballerina with a spark of intelligence. Her name was Natalie Warner.

When she came by the house a few weeks later, after they had started dating, Harriet fussed over her, commenting on her slim, curvaceous figure and Natalie turned beet red, a shade that's a bit too red. As our first dinner guest in years, Natalie explained her reticence by saying that she was deeply religious. But her lightness and laughter whenever she was around Jeff suggested otherwise, like she was another person. Jeff decided that Natalie was perfect. I was not so sure. Something about her seemed too tentative and uneasy, like a beautiful bird tweeting too loudly in a cage and concealing a broken limb. But then I was known for being too cautious and thinking the worst, not the best, of someone, and in any case, it was too late—Jeff Thurman was in love. He'd already met her family, he told us. He matter-of-factly informed us that Natalie was the daughter of U.S. Senator James Warner.

Jeff added that he thought the Warner family was strange and elusive, and he said he wasn't sure why; but he also said he was prone to asking why about everything, and he figured that Natalie's family's strangeness may have had something to do with the fact that Jeff didn't have brothers and sisters and living birth parents. After all, he said, and he was right, his own was an unusual family background and, therefore, he reasoned, anything normal (for other people) struck him as unusual. Jeff concluded that his concerns were marginal and quite possibly unfounded.

We all started paying more attention to Senator Warner. I read the newspaper before my morning rounds and would hunt for any mention of him in the news. Harriet would bubble up and erupt every time she saw him on the television as though he was part of the family. Ned, the ranch groundskeeper, would find a way to work in a reference to "Jeff's girlfriend's senator father" during our daily discussions. It wasn't that I didn't trust Natalie or her family. It's just that I didn't know them.

Jeff was getting to know Natalie. So was I.

That summer, on break from his studies and her dance tour, Jeff and Natalie went hiking and snorkeling off the coast at Catalina Island. They traveled to the nation's capital, visited Congress and toured the senator's offices. They met the Vice-President for lunch with Senator and Mrs. Warner. It was a whirlwind of excitement around the house as we tracked the couple's itinerary through letters, postcards, phone calls and newspaper clippings. After Jeff and Natalie returned from Washington, it seemed like they were always packing for a day trip to the beach, a weekend in Las Vegas or a drive up the coast to Santa Barbara. There wasn't a bit of trouble. He seemed happy the whole summer, his semester behind him and better days ahead and a beautiful dancer by his side.

By the fall, the senator, his family and any lingering concerns seemed utterly superfluous. When his classes resumed, Jeff studied with a stronger sense of purpose. He proposed marriage on New Year's Eve. They eloped the next day, January 1, 1994. Ned, Harriet and I stood with most of the staff and their families and waved to them as the taxi pulled away and disappeared down the winding road toward the airport for their flight to a honeymoon in Bermuda. They returned a week later with a suntan and announced that they planned to live at the ranch until they found a home of their own. Harriet burst with a yelp at that news and carried on like an overzealous grandmother twittering about where to put the babies until I told her to cease the silliness and get back to balancing the books or there might not be any babies.

A short time later, while lying in bed one night, I was making mental preparations to convert the master bedroom, in which I'd been sleeping, into a full suite. I needed a larger bathroom with a vanity for the ballerina bride, Mrs. Jeff Thurman. It was then I heard the sounds of another nightmare.

Natalie was asleep in their bedroom with the door closed, and Jeff had been up all night working on one of his theories and had fallen asleep on the couch. This time, Harriet was already there when I arrived. He was up and awake and talking excitedly. Apparently, he had had another premonition involving widespread destruction, as he had dreamt over 20 years ago before the 1971 quake. Jeff grabbed the phone to warn Cal Tech's seismologists, who of course thought he was delusional—but, the next day at 4:31 a.m., a major earthquake occurred, resulting in collapsed freeways, buildings, apartments and parking garages. Gas mains ruptured, fires burned, and many died in the disaster.

In Jeff's nightmares there indeed appeared to be an element of premonition. After the tremblor, Jeff was disturbed for weeks. Harriet and I speculated about what else in his dreams might come true—he had dreamt of strangers and gunshots in the dark, a child screaming, and towers burning with alarms and sirens wailing. But Jeff was too busy preparing for life as a scientist, developing theories about black holes, sunspots and spatial relationships in anticipation of his work for NASA at JPL. And Natalie, who had resumed her tour with the Tantham Ballet. After obtaining his Ph.D., Jeff's life was just beginning.

Or so he had reason to believe.

Chapter 5: Choices

In the year 1995 Jeff Thurman had good reason to believe life was very close to bliss. He had a beautiful home, a wife he loved as his equal, and his work for NASA was rich and stimulating. One of those was not as it appeared. Another was much more.

Jeff's days were filled with the task of finishing his studies and testing his thoughts on theories. He'd taken his father's furious notes and assorted contraptions to the lab for further study and examination. From what Jeff said he could tell, they might be useful in developing his ideas. He spent hours in the lab thinking, experimenting and building models.

For a long time, it seemed that he was making progress toward establishing black hole connections. He'd come home late at night and tell Natalie and I that he wasn't sure exactly what would come of these tenuous connections, but he was convinced that they could lead to some discovery for human progress and he was determined to find out. Then, there would be stretches of time with no advancements. Nothing. Only discouraging comments from colleagues and professors. He'd look down at dinnertime for days, or scratch his chin and furrow his brow, but he never acquired that constantly bothered look that had plagued Theodore Thurman. He kept at it, but he did so happily and masterfully.

Suddenly, months later, Jeff would achieve a minor breakthrough, and he would drive out to some remote part of southern California—the mountains, bluffs or desert—to set up telescopes, travel to nearby facilities, meet with visiting scholars and read classic works by Galileo, Copernicus and Newton. Then, he would be encouraged again. The cycle would repeat, back and forth, like a pendulum. No answers—bursts of enlightenment—more dead ends, this was the scientific process. Jeff was a dogged, confident scientist, painstakingly working out suppositions and propositions, reworking them after failure, and getting back to business—toiling until the pink of pre-dawn. He was resolute.

Living temporarily at the ranch house with a husband who worked into the wee hours, Natalie Thurman was a model for patience and understanding. One time, Jeff fell asleep, his head on his arm, at the dining room table where he was testing an idea using a Bunsen burner. Jeff's arm jerked, knocking the burner over. It rolled to the floor, where the flame licked a nearby curtain. Smoke set off the alarm, but not before part of the dining room caught fire.

Jeff might have slept through it, had his bleary-eyed bride not come from the bedroom, and, upon finding him asleep at the table in the flickering light of the house fire, retrieved a fire extinguisher from the kitchen. Calmly but insistently, she pushed Jeff aside with her elbow, aiming the hose toward the dining room window, and doused the flames. By morning, Natalie was ordering new curtains and making breakfast, with not a word about Jeff's work habits. All she said was: "Did the experiment get results?"

I had to admit that I thought Natalie was a perfect match, partner and companion, as precise and driven as Jeff. They were two of a kind, striving for the best without a thought to short-term pain. In work and at play, Jeff and Natalie Thurman made the most of it.

During much of that first year, Natalie traveled with the ballet. They kept in touch through written correspondence and, mostly, telephone calls to and from her hotel rooms. Natalie called every night from the road.

"Hello, Darling," Jeff answered one night when she phoned from the tour.

After the dance performance, her spent body ready for rest in the hotel room, she said, "Hi". Out of breath, Natalie exhaled. "I miss you." She paused, "and Mabus and everyone at Thurman Ranch." She laughed at herself. "Even Harriet."

Jeff smiled as he lay back on his bed, asking about the tour, taking in the sounds of his wife's soft voice as she unspooled.

"Everyone in the company is tired—tired of being yelled at. We're all nearly sick of ballet," she chuckled. "I'm exhausted, night after night, and no one is having fun right now. The reward is the dancing, but I have to admit that tonight I'm counting the days until we're back in Los Angeles." He closed his eyes, letting Natalie's words sink in, one hand on the phone, the other behind his head. He listened. He imagined her moving in perfect motion to the music.

"Tonight, I almost tumbled out of a pirouette. I caught myself and regained control. I mean, I think I'm doing good work. I know I can do better." She paused, smiling and turning as she lay on the hotel bed, pushing a strand of long, brown hair out of her eyes. "Jeff," she said, lowering her voice, "I thought of us on the beach in Bermuda. I daydream about it during rehearsals. At night I can almost feel your body's rhythm with the tide coming in around us." She told him: "I love being married to you."

Jeff pictured her in silk sheets, her body begging him to touch. Natalie, pent-up with desire and bubbling up from under, told him more. "We're going to be so happy together," she declared. "We'll get our own place and we'll make a space for your experiments, maybe a room for barre practice. We'll do everything right." She went on, building herself into a kind of tense, excitable fury—a romantic yearning for a beacon. She told him she wanted to prepare his dinner, wash and press his shirts, and brew fresh coffee for late night work projects. When she got around to planning a second honeymoon, Jeff stopped her.

"Natalie," he said, "daydreaming can cost you the season," he said, trying to be stern and smiling on the inside. Being unaccustomed to expressions of admiration—and ready to receive it—he couldn't help but laugh. "I wish you were here, too." His voice was easy, reassuring. Jeff knew it was difficult for newlyweds to be separated. He sensed that a couple working in professions such as ballet and physics hadn't much room for nuance, let alone error. He wanted Natalie to know that he wanted her very much.

He told her: "We will make ourselves happy."

"I'll be home soon," she whispered in reply, pushing her hair behind her ear and stroking her lobe along the way, feeling warm and vulnerable at the sound of his voice, as her roommate emerged from the hotel bathroom and walked into the room. "In—seven—weeks," she haltingly said, as if to herself, counting on her fingers. "After Mother and Daddy come to see my last show in Washington."

Finally, she inhaled.

"How are your studies?" Natalie asked breezily, turning businesslike and changing the subject, knowing the answer.

"Fine," Jeff said. "I scheduled time with my professor to go over calculations. I think he might help with something."

Natalie's roommate settled into bed and gave Natalie a look. "Jeff, I have to go, or else Regina will report me to headquarters. Put her on the list." They had an inside joke; an imaginary list of people they would banish to the dark side of the moon.

Jeff chuckled, closed his eyes and listened to her voice one last time. "We'll talk tomorrow," he said. "I'll be home from the lab by eight. Call me then."

"Jeff?"

"Yes?"

"I'm happy knowing I'm your wife."

He smiled from ear to ear, a handsome smile. "I love you, Natalie". The words rolled off his tongue. He ended with: "Goodnight, Natalie." "Goodnight, Jeff."

They went on like that for weeks, teasing and playing like kittens, and sometimes more like strong, sinewy cats, until she returned and they started to plan the next phase of their lives. They decided they would live near her parents and Cal Tech, in San Marino or South Pasadena, considered seriously the prospect of having kids, probably two, and sending them to private schools. Jeff would work in the lab, Natalie would dance, at some point they both might also teach, and they would visit Senator and Mrs. Warner in Washington in the spring and spend weekends at Thurman Ranch, where their kids would learn to pick oranges, read stories aloud by the fire and ride wild horses. They'd asked me to run the ranch.

Everything sounded perfect; it was the California dream, really, and no one could tell Jeff and Natalie otherwise. Jeff had kept to himself. He didn't have friends, except for a fellow grad student from India who came over to study once in a while, and he didn't have anyone else other than Ned, Harriet, the ranch hands and me. When I voiced my wonder over whether things seemed too good to be true, Jeff brushed me off.

I'd probably have brushed me off, too. By the time Natalie had returned from touring with Tantham, my concerns had abated. The worry had eased. Clearly, they were in love, spending every spare hour together, lounging on weekends for cookouts and chores. Natalie sometimes woke before dawn, rolled up her sleeves and went out with Ned for hours while Jeff went over accounts with Harriet. They didn't lack for time together. Whether driving up to San Francisco during a break or stealing time for a drive to Senator Warner's cabin at Lake Arrowhead—her father didn't know Natalie had a key—they were a happily married couple and I know that's not an easy state to achieve. I can't honestly say I ever saw Theodore and Jenny as happy as their son was with his darling Natalie.

Natalie was relaxed at Thurman Ranch, making lemonade or chopping vegetables and peeling potatoes with me in the kitchen, or helping Harriet fold the laundry, talking about her favorite choreographers, composers and music. One time, while washing freshly picked oranges in the sink, she asked about Jeff's upbringing.

"It is so remote here," she said evenly, "and there were no siblings, no playmates, no mother. Was he lonely, Mabus?"

I paused for a few moments and I thought about Natalie's question. "I suppose you'd have to ask Jeff. We kept him pretty busy around here, you know," I replied, noticing how Natalie held herself upright in the posture of a dancer, even while washing oranges. She nodded, the corners of her mouth in permanent upturn, still in her honeymoon gauze. "There was always something to do. He didn't have a lot of idle time," I said, looking toward the rocky hills in the back of the house. "He used to play cowboys and Indians up on the rocks when he was a boy."

I wanted her to know what she seemed to want to know—though something about her question seemed to come from far away. I have to say that I think I'd hoped that by telling Natalie more about Jeff I'd find out more about Natalie.

"I don't think playing alone inhibited him," I concluded. "Jeff often wound up bringing back some critter, or reporting the discovery of a rock formation. Or he was off again to perform an experiment in nature, which he had described breathlessly over lunch in advance. In fact, I think he was six when he started keeping a log about his observations."

Natalie had stopped what she was doing. The water was still running. She was looking right through me, as if she was in another world. "He was so free as a child," she said.

"I think so," I said, thinking she was delivering a high compliment and trying not to be boastful.

But, then, I sensed a kind of withdrawal. Natalie had receded, she was drifting away and soon she was far in the distance. "He was loved," she muttered to herself, and I suddenly became aware that her comment hadn't been about Jeff as much as it had been about Natalie. "He was left alone." Her words had a finality that sent a chill down my spine.

"Well, Jeff didn't always *want* to be alone, Natalie," I explained, trying to re-establish the context as a conversation about her husband and show her that he, too, hadn't always been loved. "He used to run up to his dad with a toy or a video game, and he'd want his dad to play with him." I wanted to tell her that I didn't think Jeff was loved at all—not by his father—but it was too late; I'd lost her. She had what she apparently thought she needed. Now, the best part of her was gone.

That night at supper, Jeff pulled Natalie close after they had finished their desserts, and she seemed to be positively reattached to reality. Jeff had that effect on everyone. If you were down, or drifting into dwelling on something, he would act swiftly, as if his own lack of a childhood to call upon helped him to draw on his confidence and intelligence to pull you out of the cave or down from the clouds. He'd say something kind, he'd say it strongly, and he'd say it with a certain spark in his eyes that told you he knew exactly what he was doing—he knew you knew it, too—which was pulling you out of a tailspin. He made Natalie feel that way. Like she belonged on Thurman Ranch. Like she belonged here on earth.

Tender, tenuous Natalie breathed, relaxed, and bloomed whenever Jeff was nearby. But I couldn't help but wonder why she'd be prone to shut down in the first place. It happened on occasion, like an inward drift toward darker thoughts, triggered by something someone said or did. Such moments were an exception, not the rule, and they were easy to miss. So it was hard to take her drifts seriously. Especially when Jeff and Natalie's future seemed so bright.

By now, you've probably figured out that it isn't—or wasn't—and, if you have, you're right. As Jeff and Natalie's life planning became more serious, the house hunting began, with standard mortgage pre-qualification and meetings with real estate professionals, and I think that's precisely the time when Jeff and Natalie spun into different orbits. He was actively engaged in mapping their future. She was decidedly not; the closer to buying a house they came, the less she was interested. It's as if there was an unseen obstacle in the way. No one but Natalie knew why.

Jeff, wrapping up studies—we all attended the graduation ceremony when he received his Ph.D.—was oblivious to the drift as he charted his career at JPL. He couldn't afford to be distracted, even for a few hours, though I know that he must have been aware on some level that they were drifting apart. Jeff later told me that he thought that this was merely their period of adjustment. Natalie experienced sudden and dramatic mood swings. She began eating too much, then, just as abruptly, she was not eating at all, and she'd make a fuss over having a salad. She would minimize skipping a meal, make a fuss over the minimizing, and then later I'd find her in the kitchen, rummaging through whatever was in the refrigerator—and she'd make a big deal out of minimizing that, too. She gained ten pounds—which is a lot for a ballerina—and I noticed that she became hostile in an instant at the most trivial subjects. Natalie was unpredictable.

One day, she snapped after coming home from rehearsal. She had learned that Harriet had scheduled a day off and she flew into a rage, railing against Ned, Harriet, me and everyone at Thurman Ranch. I asked her if something else was wrong. "Lately, you seem agitated," I said.

For a second, she looked like a cornered wild beast about to pounce for the kill—and then she retreated. "I'm tired," she groaned. "I've been practicing for next season and Mother's been on me about starting a family," she said, her voice going low and its tone sounding down. "Daddy wants me to have children. He wants me to be the lead dancer. Daddy wants me to make campaign appearances. I need to be with my father during his campaigns. You don't understand, Mabus. Daddy means everything to me. I have to perform. You don't understand. I don't expect you to get that I'm my daddy's sugar pie. I have to be there, it's my duty, he needs to have me there."

She went on, sounding small and defensive and not contrite. It wasn't like Natalie. She was a wreck. Something was eating at her. So I said what I was thinking out loud.

"If I may say so, it sounds like you're preoccupied with something that's upsetting you," I said.

"I'm not upset" she snarled, practically spitting the words, "so back off." She'd popped like a pistol. I did. I let the moment settle in and I later let it go, but not without mentioning the conversation to Jeff when he came home from the lab.

He sat there for a long time, puzzled, unable to calculate the meaning of her behavior. "She's under a lot of pressure, Mabus," he finally said, trying to convince himself. "I'm sorry she snapped at you like that. I'll try to ease the burden."

Jeff's efforts failed. Within months, Natalie showed signs of severe depression. She was pulling further away, alternately attacking Jeff or shoveling food into her mouth, and sometimes locking herself in the guesthouse, which she used for exercise and practice. When Jeff's entreaties failed to reach her, Natalie often fled the ranch and retreated to the Warner family's estate in Pasadena, where she'd spend the night. The union was disintegrating.

Jeff tried to reconnect, pleading with her to get counseling, giving Natalie space, and trying every approach he knew to make their marriage work. He sent flowers, he found a therapist, he listened to her for hours. But without knowing what was at the root of her sadness, or frustration, he was powerless. Within 24 hours of the worst episodes, she'd come running back to Jeff full of apologies, only to repeat the cycle. Fall apart, flee to Daddy, return to Jeff, apologize profusely. That was the pattern. She was torn, tormented and confused. No one, it seemed, could help. Only Natalie knew the answer.

We'd failed to reach her. Finally, after a few wonderful weeks of uncharacteristic calm and sobriety, she came apart. It happened on a Wednesday at the ranch. Jeff was at the lab, Harriet was in the garden, and I was painting at my easel, where I could hear a violin solo rising from the guesthouse, where Natalie had gone for her morning ballet practice. I heard a sudden "pop!" and I turned. As I did, I saw Harriet barreling toward the guesthouse. I think I felt my heart stop.

I ran toward the guesthouse, finding Harriet standing in the doorway, stricken with horror. Natalie's body was in a contortion against the mirrored wall of her makeshift ballet studio, her face pressed against her mirror image, blood trickling from the hole in her temple, the mirror shattered and splattered with a crimson blot, and a smoking gun perched in her lifeless, upturned palm.

She had killed herself with a single shot to the head.

After the initial shock, trauma and pain subsided, Jeff shut down. Having lost the most important women in his life—his mother during his birth, his wife during what was supposed to be his rebirth—Harriet and I were deeply concerned about him and we urged him to get some grief therapy. Eventually he did. Widowed in his prime, having had what he thought was a blissful marriage, which had instead spiraled out of control, Jeff was despondent. Natalie left no note, no clues and no explanation. Only a damaged, confused husband.

The strange funeral was another mystery. Senator and Mrs. Warner insisted on a religious burial, which Jeff, unsure about what she would have wanted, agreed to, and the tension was thick and aggravating. Natalie's family—father James, mother Arlene, brother Mike Warner—were stone-faced. However, Mike seemed to be suppressing a great deal of anger, and curiously so at that. One by one, members of the Tantham Ballet corps expressed condolences to Jeff, tossing a pair of Natalie's ballet slippers into the ground as the senator's family lowered the casket while press photographers unleashed a last elegy in camera clicks and final floodlights of flashes and the cold, dark death sermon was delivered. One by one they left.

Ned, Harriet and I stayed with a cluster of Thurman Ranchers at Jeff's side to comfort him. We'd been through this before, over 30 years ago, when Jeff was a newborn. Now, he stood close to his dead wife, blinking once, when Senator Warner shoveled dirt into Natalie's grave, and I could see that Jeff was trembling. I think he was on the verge of a breakdown.

He didn't speak for days. Then weeks. When wrecking crews and a bulldozer showed up a month later, I knew the bloodstained guesthouse was about to be razed. When the structure had been destroyed, and the guesthouse was gone, Jeff stood before the sliding glass doors, staring at the vacant spot, and, finally, he spoke. "I missed her clues," he said. "I didn't know she was driven to die."

He said he could solve the problems of the universe—but he was helpless to see what hurt his wife. I listened. I wondered whether the Thurman women— and their men—were cursed.

The year passed. Days were slow, long and painful. Harriet removed the framed wedding photos, I put Natalie's things in storage and Jeff begrudgingly let us carry on with the business of the ranch. He went to work, usually in a daze. He tried to adapt. With therapy once a week, and new work at the lab, he had plenty to do. Months went by with no one saying a word. I got used to the sound of clinking dishes, tweeting birds, and country music from Harriet's bedroom.

When we brought a pup home from the local animal shelter, Jeff managed a half-smile, but he was not ready to bond. I named the fluffy thing Stanley, but Jeff was having none of Stanley and our obvious attempt at boosting his spirits. One night, while doing a minor kitchen repair, I heard muffled sounds coming from Jeff's room. Thinking that the nightmares had returned, I opened the door and stepped in, only to find him sitting in his reading chair softly sobbing, with Stanley nestled in Jeff's lap looking terribly concerned. Without a word, my son held up his hand. I bowed, backed away and closed the door.

I never saw Jeff cry again.

That winter, as things were getting less mournful, a large, expensive car pulled up in the driveway and out came Natalie's brother. Mike was taller than his late sister and just as thin, with gray at the temples of his dark brown hair. I think he was a corporate lawyer or something and I wondered what he was doing here. By the time he'd made it to the door, Harriet had flung it open, thrown herself at him and trapped the poor man in a bear hug. He gave me a pleading look, so I stepped in, took his coat, offered him a drink and showed him to the living room. I asked Mike Warner what we could do for him.

"I need to speak with Jeff," he said flatly, sounding as though some issue had been resolved and this visit was its resolution. "Is he in?"

I could see that Mike was still stricken with grief. Natalie was his only sibling. We all knew he'd been hit hard by the loss. Mike was seated on the edge of the sofa. He was as nervous as Natalie used to be whenever Jeff wasn't around. Something about him seemed different, though. I sent Harriet to make a pitcher of iced tea with lemon while we waited for Jeff to return from an exercise run on a nearby trail. We talked for a while. Mike worked at a major law firm downtown. He asked about the ranch. I asked about his family.

Jeff entered through the glass doors in the back and went for the kitchen, noticing Mike Warner immediately.

"Mike," he said cheerfully, sizing him up. "It's good to see you."

"Hello, Jeff," Mike said solemnly, almost apologetically, dabbing his eyes. "May I have a word in private, please?"

"Yes, of course. Let me just change and I'll meet you on the terrace. Mabus," he said, turning to me, "will you bring us something to eat?"

And so it began that Mike Warner, liberated from the shroud of family secrecy by his sister's death, disclosed to Jeff that he and Natalie had been abused by their father.

He spared no detail. The abuse was inflicted by the senator early and often over the years, well into Natalie's and Mike's teenage years—Mike was two years older than Natalie—and he said no one knew about the physical and sexual abuse except the family, including his mother, Arlene, who would periodically walk in on Senator Thurman molesting or raping his daughter or son, and possibly a family friend named Eleanor—with whom Senator Warner seemed to spend a lot of time.

Jeff listened carefully well into the night, as the two men sat under the dark sky, sorting through Natalie's agonizing life. Mike said that he and his sister never discussed the abuse openly—it was forbidden, in compliance with the family code of secrecy—and, through the years, Mike sought therapy, went to law school, and distanced himself from his prominent family, while Natalie, he said, carried the shame in her soul. Jeff asked questions, Mike gave answers, and I, having sent Harriet and everyone out of the house for the night, served them all night with dinner, drinks and whatever else they needed.

At midnight, Jeff stood up, thanked Mike for his candor and courage, and walked him to the front door. They embraced and pledged to stay in touch, newly cemented in their common interest: the aftermath of what had been a tragic life.

As he returned to the house, Jeff looked at me, asked me to sit down and told me that he had finally understood what his father had gone through in losing his mother. To lose the love of your life, to be so filled with sadness, remorse and anger, to push everyone and everything you've loved aside because the one thing you cherished most is gone. Even being as brilliant as you are, you have no way to fix or prevent what's broken or lost—that is nearly unbearable. But Jeff told me—and he told me everything that Mike had told him—he had decided that he was not going to make the mistake his father did and suffer.

One day after Mike Warner's visit, Jeff took me to lunch and told me everything he had in mind. Psychotherapy had helped, he told me, and, step by step, Jeff said he was in recovery. He was different, he was more accessible. He became more expressive, more focused. Jeff didn't seem sad anymore—he seemed happily obsessed. He delved into his work. He played with Thurman Ranch children and took Ned to the rodeo and Harriet to a hoedown.

He also began to take Mike to dinner. The two would go rock-climbing and windsurfing and then dine at the best restaurants. Mike's friendship was good for Jeff; he got out of the lab and out of the house and he started to enjoy life outdoors again, reconnecting to work in a serious, productive way. Striving with renewed energy to correlate solar, seismic and nuclear activity, developing theories of a black hole connection, Jeff was invigorated by new knowledge. Day by day, I noticed that he transformed himself into a dynamic and driven scientist. His new lawyer pal, Mike, like his late sister, was exacting and goal-oriented. The two became best friends.

While Jeff returned to studying the physics of reality, Mike contemplated suing Senator Warner, discussing the matter with Jeff during long visits to Thurman Ranch. But, after many confidential meetings and conversations, and hiring a private investigator, Mike made the choice to dismiss a lawsuit from further consideration.

The private detective had informed Mike that the powerful senator had already grown suspicious of his son's loyalty. Senator Warner, he reported, had an accomplice named Eleanor Jones, a society matron who was rumored to be Senator Warner's mistress. Ms. Jones, the private eye explained, had taken preventive measures on the senator's behalf, including obtaining medical records of Mike's therapy and paid eyewitness accounts to Natalie's depression and he said that the senator or Eleanor Jones had met with powerful criminal types and their hacks who could threaten Mike and testify on behalf of the senator. He would ultimately be exonerated, and Mike and Natalie would be the ones disgraced.

"I'm trapped," Mike explained to Jeff after meeting with the private investigator, "I want justice for what my father did. But I won't risk my career."

"Don't worry, I will," Jeff replied, walking Mike to his car.

"How?" Mike asked.

"Leave that to me," came the reply.

Jeff got to work.

After years of research, Jeff knew what he was doing. Using his position at JPL, Jeff accessed computers and, without compromising current research projects, discreetly adjusted some of the world's largest telescopes toward what he suspected was a black hole. After confirming existence of the black hole, which he had concluded was smaller than his previous calculations had indicated, Jeff started to investigate certain possibilities and experiment with whether he could channel energy to access a space/time continuum. This would allow him access to a conduit between parallel timelines and physically travel backward in time long enough to reconstruct certain events. He went for a drive every other night after work at Cal Tech, traveling to his secret lab's clandestine location.

Working in his office at home and testing in the lab at all hours, he devised a theory for time travel. When his obsessive behavior became impossible to ignore, he disclosed and explained to me, enlisting this old man to assist in the act. It took long, grueling hours of work over several months, and our efforts required utmost secrecy amid enormous cups of coffee. Using parts of his father's machines—Jeff finally built what would be best described as a contraption, erected inside an abandoned barn on the edge of the ranch.

Jeff gave detailed instructions and, finally, he handed me a map, an overcoat and a list of certain items and locations. I had to study the list and instructions for weeks and Jeff had me practice in drills over and over and again. We finally gussied up an old Thurman Ranch delivery truck formerly used for dairy products. Taking the transport contraption out for a spin, we tested a few objects, sent them into the past. Once I'd recovered most of the objects from remote, charted locations, we advanced to the next step. It was time to test Jeff's machine with a live subject—to test a traveler in time— to save Natalie, Mike and the best of what Jeff Thurman loved about the world.

Chapter 6: Transport

The senator from California sat in a large, leather easy chair smoking a pipe, a martini perched at his side on an end table. An ashtray made of smoked glass was filled with charred tobacco, and the black and white television crackled above a low hum while James Warner drank, watched and puffed on a pipe. A curtain moved, a gun appeared, and a single shot erupted with an audible pop.

The bullet hit in the middle of the senator's forehead. His head bobbed back and forth and he slumped into the chair as though he'd fallen asleep—the pipe tumbling and coming to rest on his left trouser leg. A burst of laughter came a moment later from the television set during an episode of *Father Knows Best*.

By the time news broke that the junior senator from California had been found dead by an aide who'd arrived for a conference, a police detective named Roy Harris and his partner Earl were on the case, investigating whether the gunshot between the senator's eyes was an accident, murder or suicide.

It was late fall 1959.

Compared with science fictional time machines, Jeff's is not especially striking. It doesn't require a warp drive. It doesn't use a bank of lasers. It doesn't fling open at will or remain active for extended periods of time. It is above all a machine in accordance with nature, with more than a little help from Jeff. This next part of the story is about what Jeff did with it—not its mechanics—but I must say it's a masterful piece of machinery. The thing deserves its own tale.

So, before we continue, here it is.

Jeff Thurman's time machine is a combination of several products based on facts, certain theories and his thinking in terms of calculations, suppositions and observations. Jeff had studied a perfect scenario for a particular alignment that only works at specific points in time. Creating the device, or wormhole transport, requires enormous amounts of energy condensed into what amounts to a small tube in the time/space continuum at both ends. Think of it as two funnels with a rubber tube connecting them together. A wormhole has always been thought to exist between two black holes connected through the space/time continuum. This is because it is perceived that only black holes generate the massive amount of energy required to open a portal at both ends. However, Jeff came up with his device by taking advantage of conditions found favorable on earth.

The machine's effectiveness relies inextricably on what Jeff calls quantum singularity or what's commonly known as a black hole—energy compressed so tightly that the gravitational pull redounds to a force field of raw, incredible power—and an infinite, spinning mass that no light or matter can escape, beyond which is called the event horizon, a bluish area surrounding the black hole at the point of no return. A black hole functions very much like a toilet bowl or sink when water travels through it. As the water spins ever downward, a large amount is compressed into a small opening. There is a force pulling it down faster and faster, but only so much can go through at any given moment. So, a certain amount is ejected upward, also known as Cherenkov Radiation. This is evident if you don't have a sink guard over a garbage disposal when you turn it on or put the toilet seat down when you flush it. This has been called the "Aerosol Effect." It is an oversimplification, but for a layman like me, it works. "Old School" mainstream Astrophysicists would dismiss this description, stating that space is a vacuum and, therefore, has no place in the physics of it. But when matter (gas, liquid, and solid) all become compressed and super-heated, it becomes a plasma and, therefore, atomized like an aerosol. Matter and energy erupt from the black hole in an undulating, outward jet streaming with radioactive energy escaping from the center of a spiraling vortex.

Because a black hole spins and is massive and has its own gravity, it generates its own poles like the earth or the sun. For these purposes they can be described as north and south, with byproducts or backsplash of the burst of sustained, emergent energy.

The sun, in comparison, is much smaller and is not thought to be capable of the same extraordinary feat. However, it is what a black hole once was: an antithesis born from hydrogen gas into a ball of fusion nuclear reaction. As a star such as our sun burns out, it gives way to heavier elements until the fuel is near exhaustion and explodes. What remains can be any number of things from an interstellar red giant or white dwarf to a pulsar. One of these ultimately forms a black hole.

During the course of its life the sun reverses its north and south poles every eleven years in what is known as the solar flare cycle. When this occurs, massive solar flares erupt from the sun's surface, sending vast amounts of energy and particles into earth's path. This is called a coronal mass ejection and within eight minutes of the event's initial electromagnetic pulse (EMP), gamma rays and x-rays hit earth's Van Allen belt and are mostly deflected by the field. Hours later, vast amounts of particles hit the earth.

The earth, in turn, tries to absorb as much of this energy as possible. This release weakens earth's Van Allen belt, allowing more matter and particles to enter into the upper atmosphere. The earth generates the Van Allen belt or electro-magnetic field (EMF) because it has a metallic molten core with cooler, outer layers that spin at different rates. The earth, in essence, is a giant dynamo. This spinning creates not only earth's north and south poles, but the spinning emanates this field which protects us from outer space. Particles and elements that reach earth's atmosphere from the sun are charged and, because of the makeup of earth's atmosphere, they mix and appear as the greenish glow of the Aurora Borealis, the same type of glow visible during a trip through one of Jeff's time machines.

At the same time, many things near and on earth can and do start to fail. Utility power grids, acting as giant antennas, gather this energy and, overstressed, start failing as transformers blow and wires arc. Some of this energy is sent back along the grid to generators, including nuclear reactors. Satellites can be affected and damaged. Communications are interrupted.

Jeff had researched the nuclear reactor failure at Santa Susana Field Laboratory in 1959 and the failure at Idaho Falls in 1962. Based on historical records and his father's research at the time, he theorized that the nuclear reactor began to heat due to a bombardment of energy released from the sun and/or a nearby black hole. Many have speculated that there is more mass present in the solar system in the form of other planets besides those currently accounted for. Some have dubbed this Planet X. They have determined this from mathematical calculations and observations of perturbations such as the irregular orbit of Pluto and Uranus. The current theory is that something massive is causing this gravitational pull. Finding Pluto as Planet X was a step closer to resolving the issue, but now that astrophysicists have rejected Pluto as a true planet, there is still unaccounted for mass. Jeff Thurman concluded that a micro black hole or MBH exists, and he further resolved that it is located somewhere just outside the solar system and, occasionally, it is aimed just right to spray the earth and sun with Cherenkov Radiation.

When nuclear reactors of the type at SSFL and Idaho Falls are operating, it creates an EMF that extends to the Van Allen belt. It punches a hole in the field extending downward much like a bullet hole in a car door, allowing a small area to open and energy to enter. This field also falls well below the earth in the space/time continuum—all the way to earth's core, a veritable dynamo of energy. It was unable to relinquish the additional demand suddenly placed on it, as power flowed back into the reactor. The EMF increased and caused a cascading reactor failure, shooting more energy into earth's core, as well as solar flare energy being drawn from the sun.

Depending on the position of the sun and black hole and which way the energy to/from earth's core is being directed, the reactor core can be moved in an upward or downward direction, creating more problems. Idaho Falls was lifted up and out, impaling a technician; SSFL was forced downward.

I know this firsthand. Jeff equipped me to take a lift, or transport, during a simulation in one of the damned things. (He built several machines). It wasn't much of an experience at first, except that when the computer-simulated solar flare erupted, releasing more energy than billions of nuclear bombs exploding, earth was temporarily without protection. During our practice, something had happened.

Jeff explained to me that earth's orbital pattern, like other planets, wobbles and spins, and at certain periods of time, rolls over until one of its poles points toward the sun, usually during the extreme orbital perihelion's summer and winter, spraying energy at faster-than-light speeds in the space/time continuum. It finds a one-in-a-million chance to connect to another massive energy source and open a worm hole. With earth's Van Allen belt weakened—and with the EMF loosening the belt from the reactor running, charged from the sun's solar flares—the space/time continuum opens.

To create time travel, Jeff made an enlarged coil, with nothing in the center to get in the way of the energy, to trigger an EMF and simulate what a nuclear reactor does. The soil below it has to have minimal metal content, which explained Jeff's soil testing. Since much of southern California is volcanic, it has a high magnetite content, but not much metal content. Most is magnetite, magma, obsidian, etc. So, it tends not to be so much of a conductor as an accelerator, similar to what nitrogen sulfide or ammonium nitrate does for TNT, the accelerant for dynamite.

Jeff further educated me that the coil would help to open the vortex portal at the other end of the wormhole. However, instead of traveling through the wormhole, the time machine goes around the interior lining of the wormhole. A small door on the side of the coils allows a single person to step inside at the precise moment. A special non-magnetic grid cage allows one to enter into a double helix-type phenomena that rotates within the wormhole, allowing anything to travel forward or backward in time without physically leaving the location. So, I knew that I was to be contained within a structure that existed back in time—or in the future—without leaving the structure.

The time machine had been simulated and tested. We put several objects through using a variety of models and methods. Then I went through. As Jeff pored over the results, it became clear that his device was the amalgamation of several factors and events. During the test, for example, I maintained the same space and travel in time. Other coils, computers, robotics, and technology allow the user to control one's position, when to enter, when to leave, and time selected, though there's more to how it works, and I must say it is terribly complicated.

Jeff understood every detail—and he took every step to put his time machine into practice. We worked tirelessly to test, re-test, and adjust every instrument to get things exactly right. The margin for error was slim and the work was painstaking. But he built it and we used it. That first live mission—with Jeff belted inside—took my breath away. What it produced literally changed the course of time. I mean, some people talk about that sort of thing and write about it in novels and history books. But Jeff Thurman built it, caused it and lived it.

That he did so to avenge an injustice brings me back to reality—and puts the science and technology in perspective. As you undoubtedly know by now, Jeff had loved Natalie. The fact is that she was gone because, for all intents and purposes, she had been damaged and practically murdered. Jeff Thurman was his wife's avenger, making a way to bring her back to life. At least that was the plan.

So, here, back again at the end of the Eisenhower era, in the age of *Father Knows Best*, was a homicide detective named Roy Harris, standing in the Warner family's driveway making notes about a senator's death and pursuing an eyewitness report of a stranger seen in the area—amid reports of a transformer explosion and a greenish glow at a nearby industrial complex. With no evidence of home intrusion at Senator Warner's property, Detective Harris dismissed the transformer incident as an unrelated electrical anomaly. His partner Earl wasn't as sure.

Publicity surrounding Senator Warner's death wouldn't let Det. Harris forget the eventually suspended but conclusively unresolved investigation, or the senator's survivors. That Christmas in 1959, Det. Harris drove out to deliver presents to the Warner home for the kids and their mother, the widow Mrs. Warner.

Over the next few months, he called on Arlene

Warner with some regularity, at first as a courtesy to follow up on the investigation, then taking her and her fatherless children, Mike and Natalie, as a favor, to the newly opened Disneyland. Det. Harris became friends with the late senator's widow. A romance developed. The young couple dated for a period of time to get past emotional entanglements, as well as to alleviate any scrutiny from the press. They married in a civil ceremony in the spring of 1963. The death of James Warner was intended to spare his children the abuse. That Mike and Natalie Warner were raised by a policeman, not a criminal, was made possible by an inventor who'd had rocket science on his mind, abiding love in his heart and a commitment to justice in his soul.

What Jeff Thurman didn't know, didn't consider, was how his actions might not only touch the Warners but also intersect with Det. Roy Harris. He could not have known how their lives might eventually collide. What comes next is that part of the story.

The Sun Sets in Time

Chapter 7: Roy

Having worked all day and all night, the police detective walked into his house at two in the morning. Stepping quietly into the TV room, he eased himself onto the sofa. It felt good to sit down on something soft. It felt better not to be on guard and responsible for solving a crime and better still not to have the weight of a changing, arguably deteriorating civilization upon his shoulders. Roy Harris reached over and placed his badge on the same spot on the end table—next to an ashtray filled with spent cigarettes scattered in a heap of ashes—where he placed it at the end of every shift. He reclined, feeling his neck muscles relax into the back cushion. He let his eyes close. He breathed, inhaling, exhaling and finally letting out a long, heavy sigh before settling into a natural respiratory rhythm. The cop was exhausted.

Drenched in sweat, which was still dripping from temples near his long, dark brown sideburns, Roy was relieved. An hour ago, he was standing with his feet planted three feet apart, pumping rounds and putting three bullets into a murder suspect fleeing from the scene of a crime after he'd called out his identification, ordered the perpetrator to stop and repeated the call. The suspect had turned, sneered and gone for his gun. That's when Roy fired.

He'd done it before. He would probably do it again. The 37-year-old homicide investigator didn't get fixated on using force like some of his buddies. But he never hesitated. His aim was sure and firing was steady, and he was ranked second in target practice on the squad. His hand resting on the firearm in its holster, Detective Harris was happy to be home from work.

His batteries recharged, he got up, walked over to the television and pulled the plastic silver knob, turning the volume to low, and he headed into the kitchen for a beer. He opened the refrigerator door and saw that Arlene had been to the supermarket. There in the middle sat a nice 12-pack of his favorite brand. He grabbed a bottle and stood by the sliding glass door, pausing to listen to the familiar southern California symphony of insects and wildlife in his backyard.

It was pitch black and the floodlights of the pool and the outdoor lighting were turned off, so Roy couldn't see the steam coming off the heated outdoor swimming pool. He drank some beer while staring into the yard, listening to the crickets, owls and whatever else was moving through the brush. His thoughts wandered to what he would do on his day off tomorrow. Roy figured he'd lather on Coppertone. Lay by the pool. Go for a swim, his favorite way of staying in shape.

For now, the Budweiser would have to do. The bottle felt good in his hot hand, the same hand that held the gun and pulled the trigger, and he walked back into the TV room, fell into a chair and gulped the brew while the Star-Spangled Banner played and the American flag waved on the screen before going to static and snow. It was the late winter of 1971. It was cold outside for L.A., and Arlene and the kids were upstairs safe and sound. Roy finished the beer, set the empty bottle down, slumped in the chair and drifted into deep sleep.

A few hours later, he suddenly woke with an earsplitting headache and flashing mental images that were some sort of premonition. The pain was unbearable. Roy sat up straight, hung his head and grabbed his temples as if to make it stop. He suffered in this state for several minutes until, in a jolt that moved the whole room like it was in the palm of a walking giant's hand, Roy reeled back into the chair when the earth began to move, shake and roll like a rogue wave.

During the tremblor, Roy sprang into action, as books, bottles and debris fell around him. Water in the swimming pool was sloshing from side to side, splashing and lapping out of the pool and around the back patio until disappearing through the rain runoff drains. He ran upstairs to help his family—Arlene, Mike and Natalie—safely out of the house. As they huddled in their pajamas in the front yard, with the quake still shaking the earth, Roy went door to door, checking with neighbors.

As the rolling subsided, he went to the unmarked Buick police vehicle parked in the Harris house's carport and he radioed into the station, reporting for duty. They told him to stay put, but Roy decided that he couldn't. This shaker was too big not to have done major damage and he knew it. As waving utility poles and lines lulled to a stop, he pulled Arlene closer and said: "I'll shut off the gas and make sure the house is in good condition," he told her. His wife nodded, a kid under each arm. "Then I'll head out and canvass the neighborhood for damages, leaks and rescues," Roy said. "Mrs. Watkins is on medication, so you might want to bring her over to stay with you and the kids."

Arlene listened, nodded and felt oddly reassured as the earthquake subsided. She'd grown accustomed to seeing her husband in a crisis and he was a master of self-control. This time, in spite of the surrounding trees, poles and cars rolling and swaying in an irregular motion, Arlene knew just what to do. Neither of them had to worry about the children. Mike and Natalie Harris—that was their last name now—were teen-aged cop kids. They were eager to assist.

"I'll bring the emergency supplies in from the garage," Arlene said, as if in answer to Roy's call for mobilization. "There are flashlights, canned goods and bottled water and powdered milk. I have plenty of first-aid kits, antibiotics and bandages."

"Dad, I—can't—get—this—valve—to—turn—off," Mike Harris called to his stepdad, turning the wrench at the natural gas at Mrs. Ramirez's house across the street.

"Hold on, Mike," Roy answered, turning to see his wife heading for the garage. "Natalie," he said, "After you get Mrs. Watkins over here continue to check on others." His stepdaughter, still in her pajamas and wearing her mother's windbreaker, inclined her head, took the flashlight and marched forth. Roy jogged over to Mrs. Ramirez's house and found Mike down on the ground on his side trying to shut the gas off.

"Here," he said to his son, crouching down and taking the wrench, "let me give it a try. Go keep Mrs. Ramirez away from the house. Make sure the pets are safe. Ask if she needs anything."

As the shut-off valve started to turn, Roy heard a call coming in on the police radio in the car. He jumped up and ran back to the carport. Half a minute later he went into the house and soon emerged with his badge and holster in hand. He looked Arlene squarely in the eye, a millisecond longer than she expected, and the word for the look in his deep blue eyes was: pride. He grabbed her slender, strong shoulders with his big paws, pulled her gently forward and planted a firm, passionate kiss on her mouth. Without another word, he was off. It was a quarter past six in the morning.

In what seemed like an instant, Roy Harris had turned off the gas to his own home and was getting in the car, settling into the driver's seat, turning the ignition and backing out of the carport. Arlene watched as he drove down the tree-lined suburban street toward whatever form of law enforcement, search and rescue operation he was called upon to perform. Suddenly, as the adrenalin-fueled excitement of the earthquake abated, Arlene Harris, widowed by the murdered Senator Warner, felt a flush of relief that this police detective had come into her life—and she felt pride that she was part of his life. Roy Harris was who he chose to be and she stood by him. She felt the full meaning of that now in the face of disaster.

Neighbors started to emerge from houses with battery-operated radios, whispering about an earthquake of a 6.6 magnitude with an epicenter in the San Fernando Valley near a town called Sylmar. The petite wife and mother stood in the chilly morning air with her daughter and son, watching her husband speed off in a Buick. For a moment, she trembled. Not for herself, not for him—she knew she had married a good cop—and not for her kids, who were turning out to be better than she could have hoped for. She trembled inside, her stomach shivering and spreading to the rest of her small-framed body, and it wasn't just the result of receded anxiety from the aftermath of the quake. The trembling was a sudden sense of something sinister rising within her from the past—a long forgotten, distant memory. Pushing strands of hair out of her face, Arlene gathered strength and composure. When she felt herself losing control, she willed herself to remember her husband's kiss.

For the rest of the day, the Harris family went on, helping neighbors, tending cuts and treating Mr. Gant's broken arm—which was busted when he was pinned during the quake by a falling cabinet in the garage—fixing doors and tagging unsafe houses. As the sun set, the disaster was more or less under control on their block of the Valley. They were exhausted. The earthquake was over. The day finally ended and everyone in their suburban neighborhood had survived. The Harris family was cleaning up.

Arlene later learned that Roy had been called to investigate a collapsed freeway overpass, where he found a crushed vehicle and rescued an injured driver. But in the aftermath of what would come to be known as the Sylmar quake, Arlene Harris never felt safer, more out of danger, or more in love with her life and her husband than she did right now. At this moment, the world felt terribly wrong—but Arlene's world felt wonderfully right.

Chapter 8: Family

In that sense, someone who was watching them knew, they were the opposite of the Warners. Senator Warner, when he wasn't entering his kids' bedrooms to have his way with them, was irritable and unfocused. His wife, Arlene, was needy and overindulgent. Their kids, Natalie and Mike, were nervous and withdrawn. The family barely spoke to each other about anything other than what would please James Warner.

None of that drove the Harris family. Roy was an unsung hero, not a famous politician, and he didn't abuse his wife and kids. Roy and Arlene were easygoing; a loving couple consumed by their own lives and trying to raise children with an emphasis on criminal justice, science and education. Their values paid off in the aftermath of the earthquake, which was like a civil defense drill made real.

When they sat by the half-empty pool that night, the four of them fatigued, spent and ready to collapse, they talked about their thoughts and feelings.

One spoke about the future.

"Mom," Natalie said, bundling herself into an old sleeping bag as the sound of sirens and helicopters faded from their immediate surroundings.

"Yes, dear," came the reply.

"I am grateful. For everything. For Girl Scouts, camping at Big Bear, teaching me to knit and sew and cook. I'm glad you married Daddy after the shooting." Her words were followed by silence, except for the sound of everyone breathing. Natalie swallowed. She looked up at the dark sky. Something made her want to say these words—especially tonight. "So, thank you, Mom and Dad. What you did made a difference today." Natalie paused. "Now, I realize that it does every day."

There was another pause, and no one said a word. Then, her mother, taking in her daughter's expression and letting it sink in, said: "You're welcome, dear." Roy laid still in his sleeping bag, listening to the exchange.

"Mom?" Natalie asked. "Can I tell you something else? I'm glad you and Dad made me take those ballet classes. I know I didn't want to at first. I wanted to play softball. But when I was helping that old couple down the street today, and I saw those old photos lying on the floor, it made me aware of how short life can be and how much there is to learn and do and become." She smiled to herself. "I really want to be the best dancer I can be—I want to do it. I want to live and really be alive."

Then came another voice.

"Mom?" It was a breaking voice—half-boy's, half-man's. It was Mike's.

"Yes, dear?"

"Me, too."

Everyone lay still in the backyard by the light of the pool for a few moments. Then Roy spoke. "Son, if you want to be a ballet dancer, you're going to have to practice." The four of them burst out laughing at Roy's reply, breaking the tension, and supplying the right amount of brevity for the Harris family to relax, settle into their sleeping bags and fall asleep for the night. Roy had insisted on staying outside—one of the exterior walls of the house had been damaged and he wanted an engineer friend to have a look at it in the morning—and, as he drifted into slumber, the thought on Roy's mind was that, while he hadn't yet avenged their blood father's murder, he had done right by Mike, Natalie and Arlene.

Roy and Arlene had raised the kids to explore, detect and discover. And they did. When Natalie was seven, not long after Senator Warner was shot, she announced over a bucket of Kentucky Fried Chicken that she would become a journalist. She declared that she wanted to discover the meaning of the universe and report it to the world on the front page. A year later, the goal of becoming a reporter gave way to becoming an astronaut—she had been watching an episode of *Lost in Space* with her brother—who would take the family on long journeys to outer space, adopt orphaned aliens, study and examine them and put on shows to entertain them. By the time she was 12, Natalie had decided that she wanted to be a doctor or a detective, because that's what smart people did—discover how to heal people and stop bad people. Something like that—but for Natalie the future was always about mining facts for life.

Ballet came slowly. Natalie was enrolled at her mother's insistence in a beginner's dance class at the age of three and she was resistant, then ambivalent, about ballet until a recital convinced her that the training had paid off. She realized that she was good. She liked being good.

In fact, when she performed and received an ovation, Natalie decided then that ballet was better than the field hockey games where few parents except hers showed up and even fewer cheered. She had been reared by her stepdad to observe, listen and study in order to detect facts and understand. So Natty, as her mom called her, immersed herself in the worlds of Tchaikovsky, Chopin and Mozart. She studied artists, as she encouraged her brother Mike to study scientists and what they made, so he could explain it to her. Natalie immersed herself and studied Fosse, Balanchine and the history of ballet. She was driven. What she lacked in grace, she made up for with sheer athletic ability. Her pirouettes were perfect. Natty was on point.

It didn't matter to her that she was shorter and had more curves than other ballerinas or that she wore her hair in a short, stubby ponytail instead of a bun during practice. Her teacher, gruff and stubbled Mr. Karoukian, would give her a piece of chocolate and tell her she was the best in class. For Natty, being the best was better than having a piece of chocolate.

"Miss Natalie Harris," Mr. Karoukian would call out at the beginning of advanced ballet class, "please lead us in the stretch."

She quietly complied, all eyes upon her, some with envy.

It's not that Natalie outgrew being a tomboy as much as that she transformed dance into sport. She became aware at last of her own power. She would soon discover the limitations of her power.

As a child, Mike, too, was an intrepid investigator. Building log cabins with Lincoln Logs, he wanted to know where the toys were manufactured, how they were made, what exactly composed the wood. Mike extrapolated Lincoln Logs to the real world, asking his mother how pioneers were able to cut down large trees, fend off or make deals with Indians and manage to make a living, too.

Outwardly, he was less goal-oriented than his sister, lingering for a time on each activity. He peppered his parents incessantly with questions about his latest childhood obsessions: whether wooden Tinker Toys would be more flexible in an earthquake than hard plastic Legos, why Barbie's measurements were less to scale than G.I. Joe's, whether Dad's car could match the equivalent-scale speed of a Hot Wheels toy car and how the metal was cast. The questions caused Arlene to insist that he go play outside and test his theories or go to the library and find answers, but in any case, get out of the house.

During one summer, his next-door neighbor Bob and Bob's dad rented a sailboat and took Mike sailing a few times. Mike would perch himself on deck at dead center and, while sailing out of the marina, calculate the length of the ropes, the texture and strength of the fibers, angle of the mast, speed of the boat and position of the sun. Mike didn't come to his adoptive father and his mother with what he wanted to be in life—he just did as he wanted. An erector set, a physician's desk reference journal, various measuring instruments, tools and utility knives were his rewards, and his room was like a laboratory. His mother gave him boys' mystery and adventure books—the Hardy Boys, dog and horse stories, *Swiss Family Robinson*—and Mike read them all. He prided himself on being smart, fit and able. For his tenth birthday, he asked his dad to take him to a crime scene. Like Natalie, he wanted to know things. And, encouraged by Natalie, he wanted to do things based on his knowledge. Unlike Natalie, he was convinced he was capable of knowing almost everything under the sun.

Arlene Harris, in contrast to Arlene Warner, took parenting seriously. She made motherhood an art. When Mike was seven, she asked Roy to start taking Mike to work—to see the forensics lab and get comfortable seeing science as part of one's everyday work, not some freak field of study for maladjusted men. Mike took to crime science. He had his nose in a microscope until he was 12. That was Arlene's influence.

That's about the age he was when he started playing strategy games, reading military history and batting around a baseball with Natalie when he wasn't studying. By this time, his nose—his whole face—was in a telescope that Roy gave him for Christmas. He read about and studied the stars and looked up words and terms and constellations in an astronomy book. If he'd heard or read about a beach or night-time murder, he asked Roy about tides and moonlight and other factors.

He was known as "Cowabunga Mike" when he hit puberty because his interest in baseball had given way to an ability to sail. Roy's partner, Earl, had a small sailboat—a snipe—at the marina and he'd take Mike out to learn the skills. Sailing the snipe came so easily that half the time at sea he was charting their course and studying migrations of schools of fish. When they'd sail past Catalina Island, Mike used weather instruments to learn wind patterns. Meteorology interested him, though it was merely a warm-up. Physics fascinated him.

At dinnertime, the kids would sit and listen to their dad talk about his homicide cases. They heard about ballistics, field reports, lab mistakes and, always, following up on leads. That was paramount.

"Any new leads today, dear?" Arlene asked when Roy sat down for dinner. "Rosemary Watkins said she heard from Bill that there's been a fingerprint match in the Salazar case."

"Nope, nothing new," Roy answered, "please pass the potatoes—thanks—but I couldn't say even if there were. It's an open case."

"Any new homicides, Dad?" Mike asked. The word 'murder' had been banished from the Harris household. "I heard something on the scanner last night. More corn please."

"No, son. That was a gang-related killing. Out of my area," Roy said, passing his son a corn on the cob. "We did make progress in the Fairfax case. I'm expecting an arrest pretty soon."

"Dad, isn't that a triple homicide?" Natty asked, cutting another piece of steak as her father nodded and chewed. "I hope they get the person who did it. Do you think it's the husband?" Her dad shrugged. "Oh, Mom," she said, changing subjects, "may I have the car on Saturday night for rehearsal?"

"I don't see why not," Arlene said approvingly, after looking briefly at Roy. "Be home by eleven."

And so it went, with a kind of nonstop mutual encouragement of everyone's projects. It took a lot to get criticized in the Harris home. There was a wide berth granted for making mistakes. It was as though they were all conducting some grand secret experiment and they were in on it together.

Mrs. Harris, who had been a librarian at a local college law school, coached girls' swimming at the Y and ran the family housekeeping and finances—so she put her skills to good use and managed to get out of the house and away from the kids. The home was her domain, though she partnered with Roy on key issues and ceded to his authority when necessary.

There was rarely a conflict or crosstalk, though Mike was once caught with a Bunsen burner in an unapproved experiment and was grounded for three weeks. Natalie had a boy/girl pool party with her friends without telling her mom one weekend when Roy and Arlene had gone to Palm Springs and that didn't go over well. She lost her driving privileges for a month. Later, Roy and Arlene decided it was time for their daughter to have a proper pool party of her own—with parental guidance. They sat in the living room playing board games while the kids partied at the pool and danced to disco music in the driveway.

"Thanks, Mom and Dad," Natty whispered to them after midnight before she went to bed. "That was the best night of my life."

"Glad you had a good time, honey," her mom said, smiling. "Goodnight."

"Goodnight, Mommy," she said, coming over to give Arlene a kiss. "Goodnight, Dad." It was his turn.

"Goodnight, Natty," he beamed, as if he'd earned a medal. "Your friends are good kids and you can have them over anytime." He added: "As long as we know about it in advance…"

Natalie smiled and gave her dad a playful shove before turning and heading to her room. "Yes, Detective Harris. See you in the morning."

They both watched their daughter—who was growing into a beautiful young woman—exit the room. A minute passed until Arlene turned to Roy. "Roll the dice," she said. "It's your turn."

So, what had been secretive and repressed with Senator James Warner was warm and open with Roy Harris as head of the family. Whatever deep-seated fears and doubts Arlene had that had festered and spread with a perverted politician had been soothed and eased in the company of the policeman. Arlene, however, never knew the difference. No one did. Except the stranger who lurked near their cozy lives. He knew.

Occasionally, a reporter would call or show up at the door and ask about the murder of Senator Warner. Each request was handled by Roy, who shooed them away in every instance, referring them to police public relations. They each had their suspect theories: Roy thought the shooter might be a mobster, or a member of a street gang—there had been threats made by both. Natalie shrugged when the shooting came up and said, "it was probably someone looking for a thrill." Mike had a complicated theory involving the transformer explosion and the mafia. Roy became tense whenever it came up and refused to discuss the matter. It bothered him that the case was unsolved. The shooting or assassination of Senator Warner was the one that got away.

For Arlene Warner Harris, her first husband's murder was a terrible act laced with something secretive, not just mysterious. There was a recurring moment in Arlene's mind. She wasn't bothered by the sporadic recall or image, and it wasn't a painful experience. In her mind, her dead husband would appear from the neck up, laughing uproariously. The image disturbed her to the point of sickness—and she sensed that something about his death was connected. Yet his murder was in the past. She had moved on. Why did the flash keep happening?

Arlene didn't dare discuss it with Roy, who had never let go of the criminal investigation and pounced on the slightest possibility of a new clue. Mike and Roy would talk by the pool for hours—Arlene would send them outside—about Senator Warner's killing; the ballistics, transformer burst, weather, Mike's conspiracy theory, Roy's and Earl's police reports. None of them knew that the clues were close—and getting closer—and would come to a startling conclusion.

When Mike was 18, he enlisted in the Navy as a nuclear engineering cadet. The Navy paid for his college tuition. Eventually, Mike would manage a fleet of nuclear-powered submarines in the Pacific Ocean. But it was on an aircraft carrier that he met a young, auburn-haired Navy officer named Patrice. They were married 6 months later and, today, they have a son of their own named is Rodger. He's exactly like his father, only his demand for knowledge is intensified by an insatiable demand for justice, which gets Rodger into trouble. Arlene and Roy live in the same house, with grandson, Rodger, living in Mike's old room while he attends classes at Cal Tech—the story of Natalie Harris took a different turn.

She became a ballerina, as she was when Jeff Thurman knew her as Natalie Warner. But she was healthier, more self-assured, more agile and oddly she seemed more vulnerable, too. Her blood father had been shot in the head, her mother and stepfather had been good parents and her brother had been supportive and brilliant. So, Natty Harris was part of a warm family in which she had been loved. But at night she thought she heard whispers, strange as it may seem, from another world—or another time. She couldn't make out what she thought she heard, and, after a visit from the ballet company's psychiatrist, she figured the whispers were some form of post-traumatic stress disorder resulting from Senator Warner's shooting. But whatever the cause, the whispers were unsettling to Natalie. They would become louder.

With Natty on tour, Mike and Patrice at sea, and Rodger bunking in his dad's old bedroom, Roy and Arlene spent their time reading, swimming and working. Arlene had taken a clerical job at an accounting firm in Pasadena and Roy was nearing retirement from the police department. On Wednesdays, he met Earl at Millie's Tavern where they played pool. Roy and Arlene went with other police couples to Dodger Stadium for games during baseball season. Life was good.

Perhaps it was too good. So, it was hardly surprising when a package arrived for Roy on a quiet Thursday morning. What he pulled out of the box was an automatic weapon with a note that read: "From someone who values your life." Aware of his own safety, and always up for solving a mystery, Roy kept the anonymous gift. He'd been feeling rather useless with kids grown and gone and his job coming to a close, so he got a charge out of it—though he chose not to tell Arlene for the time being. Roy realized that it meant he might be a target, but the gun gave him something to do. What he didn't know was that it also gave him someone to be. The rest would be up to him.

Chapter 9: Natalie

The early 1990s were frustrating for Roy. The Los Angeles riots undermined the city's police officers—who deservedly didn't have the best reputation—and made his job harder.

The trial of accused murderer O.J. Simpson didn't help. Police work in general, and being a police detective in particular, was viewed with distrust, especially among the city's black population. Since most who followed the Simpson trial concluded that he was guilty, everyone thought the Los Angeles Police Department bungled evidence, investigations and prosecutions, or, worse, choked if the accused murderer was a celebrity. Roy and his partner Earl paid the price for L.A.'s high profile cases in the 1990s. The notion of O.J. Simpson getting away with stalking and murdering his wife—protesters marched through city streets calling him *the Butcher of Brentwood.*

The murders of Ron Goldman and Nicole Brown Simpson also brought a renewed interest in unsolved murders.

By now, Roy was used to the fact that, whenever a high-profile murder happened in L.A., some reporter usually ended up knocking on the Harris family's door, peppering Arlene with questions about the 1959 shooting of Senator James Warner. He could almost hear the news producers and editors puzzling, "Say, whatever happened in the case of that senator's murder?"

He was plagued by the same question. It bothered Roy to distraction. Earl told him to let it go. But he couldn't forget young Natalie and Mike—or the look on Arlene's face when she recounted discovering that her husband had been shot—and he couldn't shake the feeling that the murder had the look and polish of a professional hit. He was convinced it had been rehearsed. "Not that again," Earl would moan over a stack of paperwork if he brought it up. Roy couldn't resist. He was determined to solve the crime before he retired.

Over the years, front page articles and TV news reports about the senator's murder had tended to explore his connection with labor unions and various campaign supporters, including a wealthy heiress named Eleanor Jones.

Mrs. Jones, in particular, held interest because she was still alive and active in politics and high society, and she was easily accessible to the press. They snapped her photograph every time she stepped out of her Westside mansion. It didn't hurt that she paused and posed with her miniature dog Koo Koo Too before the Bentley came around to take her to swanky luncheons with assorted Hollywood types.

Detective Harris and partner Earl had checked her out at the time of the murder. Eleanor Jones had been seated next to Senator Warner at a fundraising dinner with several big shots in the mid-1950s. The pair had been spotted together at regular party functions throughout Los Angeles.

Her husband, T.K. Chase, was an illegitimate son of an Oklahoma preacher. In his haste to gain the approval and credibility of others, he made a fortune on the stock market by trading international favors for Washington favors by questionable means—promising the other party more than he had in fact gained in advance. He was rarely seen on the southern California social circuit. He'd met young Eleanor, an Arkansas hillbilly whose real name was Bobbie Sue McGinty, at a revival meeting in a tent near downtown Los Angeles. They'd slipped under the tent and into the back of an Oldsmobile. They'd been together ever since.

T.K. Chase Jones spent his time in dark taverns around the U.S. Capitol and in Latin American palaces, massage parlors and cathouses. He was in Havana when Castro seized power and was rumored to have been in on the Communist revolution and made a fortune when several sugar plantations were nationalized. But Roy and Earl knew that he was nowhere near L.A. when Senator Warner was murdered.

But his wife, Eleanor, was in town. Earl and Roy drove out to see her for routine questioning at the Jones estate in Beverly Hills one day in 1960.

Roy recalled that the place had an iron gate like an old Hollywood serial. It even had a butler. Roy had pulled into the driveway, after gaining access at the gate. He rolled his eyes to Earl. They'd been to enough posh estates in their investigations and the Jones place seemed like another one run by a lonely, pretentious lady with not a lot to do. "Here we go again," he said to Earl at the time.

Something was different this time. Roy knew it as soon as he knocked on the door.

Two huge black doors creaked open. An old man bowed like they were royalty.

"Good afternoon," the butler said gravely in an accent which was part southern drawl, part New England, inclining his entire body. "My name is Spencer," he said. "I am humbly at your service. Mrs. Jones is expecting you in the tearoom, detectives." Earl and Roy had glanced at one another, handing him their hats and coats, which he discarded to a nearby servant. Butler Spencer was the color of ash. He had gray, deep-set eyes and hollow cheeks. He spit when he talked and he didn't seem to have any teeth. "Please come this way."

Spencer led them down a dusty, narrow hallway—past large portraits of Mrs. Jones and her cat, Mrs. Jones standing at the staircase, Mrs. Jones seated by the fire—seated again, this time in a meadow—and finally they reached a small room isolated from the main house. Outside the window was a large garden that seemed to envelop the exterior of the house. "Tea and sandwiches shall be served," Spencer announced as he exited, closing a pair of French doors behind him.

They stood there motionless, looking around the musty tearoom, which felt damp and cold like the inside of a crypt. Roy was about to make a crack when he saw Earl shake his head—and he spotted a small, bony white hand rise from the other side of an oversized wicker chair. "Here," a tiny voice called in a high pitch, with a faint English accent. "Detectives."

They made their way over and took a seat on a loveseat facing a wiry woman whom they assumed to be Mrs. Jones.

"My name is Eleanor Jones," she stated in long, drawn-out vowels loaded with melodrama and lingering on the end of Jones so it sounded like a zzzzzzz. "I am the person you have come to see." Her eyes were beady. Her curly hair was cut in a short, black pageboy. Her bony body was like a bent stick, protruding in places, and her tinny voice grated on Roy's nerves. She was just 34 years old.

They said hello and Roy took out his notepad and pen—and the lady dressed in blue chiffon anticipated him. "My de-uh," she said, drawing out her words, "take eh-veh-ree-thing down." She leaned forward and they could scarcely escape the scent of her expensive perfume. Her black curls falling around her chin like a raven-haired Gish sister, she looked Roy Harris straight in the eye—her eyes cutting through him. "Do not miss a single word," she instructed. "I am appalled at the death of our great senator, James Warner. I wish to do everything possible to help you in your quest to investigate this unspeakable crime against the people of California."

"Thank you, Mrs. Jones." They said in unison.

Roy picked up the pace a bit.

"Now, Mrs. Jones. How did you know the senator?" He asked.

"Well, as you must know—or you would not have come calling—I am a devout supporter of the senator's causes. I believe in his crusade against profit," she said righteously. "I persuaded my husband T.K. Chase to see to it that Mr. and Mrs. Jones are on record as donors to the senator's noble cause. We favor peace and equality. Chase is in agreement and, therefore, he made the arrangements for patronizing Senator Warner's campaign. We are after all moral people."

"When did you meet James Warner?"

"At a party, as I recall."

"When was that?"

"Oh, my de-uh, that was some time ago. Shortly after Eisenhower was re-elected, as I recall. We were seated at the same table."

"Was your husband there?"

"As I recall, Chase was in Peru at the time. He was not able to attend, as is often the case. I attended the dinner with my friend Felicity Pepperington."

"How many times had you seen, met or dined with Senator Warner? Over the years."

"Oh my. I do not recall. At least on several occasions. Let's see, there was the time I was in Washington for the Lollipop Luncheon at the Hilton. It's a benefit for hungry children." She paused and waited for a response, but the two detectives stared blankly back. "Then there was a lecture series in San Francisco for peace, and there were several church socials here in Los Angeles."

She paused again, as a batch of fur known as Koo Koo waddled in like a plump raccoon and laid down near her feet, staring up at Earl and Roy with large brown eyes that were a bit crossed. "You know," she said, lowering her shriek of a voice, "Senator Warner was a deeply spiritual man. The senator knew that Chase had been raised on faith, family and the Bible. He shared those beliefs."

"How much did your husband donate?" Roy asked, as the French doors opened and in came Spencer with a tray of sandwiches and tea.

"Oh, I'm sure I don't recall. Chase says talk of money is so crass. Now, gentlemen, kindly tell me what you want to know."

It was Earl's turn. "When did you last see Senator Warner?"

"A few weeks before the murder. I was at a soup kitchen in the slums. So was James, I mean, the senator." She went flush red and righted herself, sitting up straight while Koo Koo lifted his head and looked up at her, as if mildly bothered by the disturbance. "He was helping the underprivileged."

"Yes," said Earl. "Did you notice anything unusual—anyone strange hanging around him, any comments he may have made—or anything out of the ordinary?"

She shook her head.

Back to Roy. He nonchalantly poured a cup of tea and asked, as if inquiring about the time, "And where were you on the night of his murder?"

She glared at him. He could feel the stare. So, he looked up at her, met her glare and added: "We need to know."

"I was he-uh, at our home."

"Anyone to corroborate that claim?"

"Of course not," she said coolly. "Spencer had the night off and the servants were in their quarters. Chase was in France. I was here with Koo Koo. Frankly, I was meditating at the time in my bedchamber."

She stopped, catching her breath, and continued in a lower voice: "I heard about his terrible, terrible death on the news." Mrs. Jones closed her eyes. Sniffled. "The following day. It was everywhere. Terrible," she stated as if the world's weight was upon her. "Of course, Chase called home when he heard it, too. We prayed. I wept."

The somber moment passed and her eyes popped as she turned to the detectives, pouncing like a cat on its prey.

"When will you catch the one who murdered him, Detective Harris?"

Roy held her gaze. "As soon as we get the evidence, Mrs. Jones."

They rose to leave while she lifted a bell and rang and Spencer shuffled into the tearoom.

"And why did you say it was one, Mrs. Jones?" Roy asked.

She shrugged. "James was a man of the people. I think it must be a lone individual to have done such a terrible deed."

James. She had said it again and this time she didn't correct herself.

And that was that. For over 30 years, the sharp exchange in a Westside tea parlor had lingered in Roy's mind. He was convinced that the eccentric Eleanor Jones had been hiding something—that it was something bad—and that it somehow involved Senator Warner. He was sure of it.

As they'd exited the manor that day, with the butler trailing closely behind, Earl muttered to Roy that he didn't think they'd heard the last of Eleanor Jones. Roy's reply, within earshot of the shifty servant: "She hasn't heard the last of me."

"Good day, gentlemen," said the butler, who gave no indication of a response, drawing out his words as he bowed at the opened doors. A slight change in Spencer's expression as they passed caught Roy's attention. He followed Spencer's gaze with his eyes and noticed what looked like a small toy on the pavement of the driveway, no larger than a trinket from a box of Cracker Jack. It looked like a miniature battleship made out of metal. Roy acted if he hadn't noticed. When his eyes met Spencer's, the old man had the hint of a sheepish grin, minus the teeth.

"Do these two have any children?" He asked Earl when they got in the car.

"Yes—hers by a previous marriage, according to hospital records. They live with the father," Earl said, reading his notes as Roy drove off the estate. "Apparently, he had problems with his kids being raised by T.K. Chase Jones."

Roy had said he would check it out and he did—but when he met Eleanor's ex-husband for coffee at a downtown L.A. diner, the man refused to talk. Said he'd had enough of Eleanor Jones and he didn't want the kids dragged into any trouble. When Roy had asked about custody, though, the Ex gave a cryptic comment. "Let's just say the kids are better off with their dad," he'd said. Then he got up, shook Roy's hand, dropped a few dollars on the table and split. He was an oil executive. He seemed happy that Eleanor Jones was ancient history.

So, the trail went cold. It was a different time, Roy knew. Back then, people weren't as open, they didn't talk about things. They didn't talk about their feelings or anything perceived as remotely controversial or unusual. He always wondered about Eleanor Jones, her ex and those kids. What was she hiding? What was her angle? And what if anything did it have to do with the murder of James Warner?

Of course, we know that Roy Harris had no idea that James Warner was a pedophile who'd molested his own kids in another time, and who knows what characters he might have been mixed up with—he could have been shot by an angry parent and victim—and Eleanor Jones might have been just another strange lady with money.

Throughout her ballet career, Natalie Harris had met thousands of women like Eleanor Jones; idle, passive women of inherited wealth who had contempt for an

American middle-class work ethic. At soirees for ballet benefactors, in hotel ballrooms for fundraising luncheons, and backstage in dressing rooms, Natty had met her type many times over.

"Dahh – ling," they'd typically say, elongating their vowels, grabbing her thin shoulders and pulling her closer toward over perfumed bodies and over painted faces, "How I adore watching you dawn-ce." One glimpse from the corner of her eyes of an icy stare from the ballet director and Natty knew to smile, nod and muster a demure "Thank you, Mrs. Wellington," or some such nonsense.

There was no denying, however, that audiences did adore watching Natalie dance.

She never knew what they saw in her movements. She knew only that she heard the music, felt it sweep through her body in a single sensation, and she engaged decades of rigorous practice at Mr. Karoukian's instruction to execute the steps, leaps and pirouettes. Holding on point during the quiver of a note or leaping and extending her long legs into the air to embody the burst of music from an instrument, Natalie expended what she knew and felt in a single, swift action. By the time she'd pause to finish and turn to the audience, she could see they were typically standing, moved or even thrilled, in praise of her performance.

There had been years of touring with the ballet, throughout the 1970s and 1980s, in everything from the classic Russian ballets—*Swan Lake, The Nutcracker, Sleeping Beauty*—to *Firebird, The Four Temperaments* and *Age of Anxiety*. She had been as stunning, no, more so, as Natalie Harris than she had been as Natalie Warner. On stage, critics, peers and others observed that Natalie was poised and direct, framing the scene by her body as if the symphony's music was channeled underneath the stage in a force field transfused into her slender body.

Others danced leading roles and others were better on technical terms, but the eye always moved to Natalie. She danced the smallest parts like she was a sunbeam frolicking inside a kaleidoscope—expressing lightness, playfulness and purpose—prancing over here, then there, then racing into her partner's arms for an elevation.

Offstage, too, she was a force. Withdrawing backstage with the rest of the company, she would sit alone, decline party invitations and stare into the mirror as a void in quiet contemplation or deep examination—it was hard to tell which. It was as if after the dance everything around Natalie became an empty space. When her parents visited backstage, with her father Roy invariably carrying a dozen roses, she was young Natty again, animated, talented and aware of her skills. But soon after they left she drifted, her thoughts wandering elsewhere to the point of preoccupation, as lonely as a genius. As vibrant and alive as Natalie was on stage, she was that subdued behind the scenes.

A young dark-haired dancer named Anthony stubbornly challenged her solitude, despite discouragement from the other dancers. "Leave her alone," whispered the director, as everyone filed out late one night, peering past the others toward the solitary figure entranced by her own image. "She's no good after the curtain call."

"Go on," said Anthony simply that night, "I want to see for myself what strange Natalie is all about." He certainly wasn't moved by the prospect of romance, as he was a known homosexual who, it was disseminated, had discreetly slept with a one of the other male dancers. Besides, Natalie was known for her devotion to no one. Anthony Stefano wasn't the most flamboyant male dancer, and he had a modest female following of his own, but he had a large family of brothers and he had always wanted an older sister. For some reason, Natalie struck him as a good, safe pick.

So, that night, Anthony stood there, after the others had exited and Natalie remained seated in front of the mirror, under her nightly delusion, introspection or spell, limply brushing her long brown hair, absent an ounce of effort. The crew had packed up and departed and there they were, silent dancer and youthful male ingénue. He sat for a time reading a paperback novel. When doors started closing, she finally stopped brushing and moved to retrieve her bag. She spoke to him in a soft voice. "Don't wait for me, Anthony."

He didn't know she knew his name. She had said it as though she'd asked a janitor to turn off the lights. There was an odd familiarity about the way she'd said it.

"That," he said in answer, "is exactly what I'm going to do." He added, in a friendly tone, "and I think you know it." She paused at that, bearing a slight smile in the corner of her mouth. "Come on then," she said. And off they went, turning off lights, exiting backstage and hailing a taxi.

"Where to?" The driver asked as the door opened and slim Natalie slipped inside.

"Greenwich Village." It was Anthony's voice, and he stepped in and closed the door as Natty scooted over. "Want some gum?" he asked.

"No, thanks," she said, watching dark shapes of buildings pass by.

After several minutes, he offered: "I make the best spaghetti. Are you hungry?" She was about to say no again when, pondering some advice Mr. Karoukian had given her as a girl, her eyes widened. She turned to Anthony for the first time and said plainly, "I'd love some." "No problem," Anthony answered in a thick New Jersey accent, gobbing the wad of chewing gum he'd smacked into his mouth. "Mama gave me the recipe."

They were fast friends, like a couple of mismatched kids, the Italian kid from Jersey and the cool California girl—or the backup dancer and a leading ballerina. Their friendship raised eyebrows because no one could figure out what they had in common. It wasn't a romantic thing. It wasn't a dancer thing—they had nothing technical to learn from one another—and it wasn't a play for status, opportunity or position. He missed his family and wanted a mentor. She felt like she didn't fit in and had always wanted a kid sister. She didn't mind that the only willing participant happened to be a boy. He didn't care that she was odd. Anthony Stefano was the only one who'd waited around to get to know Natalie Harris. In their own way, the detective's daughter and the butcher's son, years apart and rarely on stage at the same time, were a good match.

He'd been born in Sicily and moved to New Jersey with his family—six brothers, his parents and all four grandparents—when he was small. He had always wanted to dance, ever since his mother took him to see *West Side Story*. He told Natalie that night over a plate of spaghetti and a bottle of Chianti in his East Village walkup that he knew he'd had a crush on Bernardo and that he'd already figured out that he might be gay. She'd known gay kids in high school, but not like this—19-year-old Anthony was her first gay friend. They talked about food, wine, dance, disco, Blondie, *Soap*, who shot J.R., and everything under the sun until she came to the topic of her biological father's murder.

"Heh," the kid sniffed, letting the notion sink in. "So, he was a Senator?" He paused and ate some spaghetti. "Sorry about your dad." Then he paused again and thought about it. "But he wasn't really your dad." Natalie knew right then she'd made a friend for life. Unfazed by the murder, the fame or the details, he zeroed in on what mattered to Natalie, who was about the same age when Senator Warner was shot as Anthony was when Papa Stefano moved the family from Sicily.

In time, as seasons passed, they hung out together and traveled to Mexico on vacation. She stayed with him in the Village, sleeping on the sofa, when they performed in New York. They went to gay bars, punk clubs and discos and strangely enough it was an anchoring experience for the girl from Los Angeles. She visited the Stefano family in New Jersey and met Mama and Papa Stefano and some of the brothers. He met her dad Roy and mom Arlene when they danced in L.A. They went to the beach, to Disneyland, lounged by her parents' pool when they weren't practicing.

As Natalie and Anthony grew closer, her parents wondered whether she, too, might not be the marrying kind. Not that it would make them love her any less.

"I don't care if Natalie is a lesbian," Roy stated openly to Arlene one night after dinner as the kids walked out to go out for a swim. "That Anthony is a nice kid and I like him. I just wish she'd find somebody to date."

"So do I, Roy," confided her mother. "I admit I'm having a tough time thinking she might be gay, though."

It was a logical plausibility, as Natalie's brother Mike would say, and working in the Navy—married to a woman enlisted in the Navy—Mike ought to know; he had learned plenty about women who were lesbian. Natalie had never shown much interest in men—she'd been a tomboy as a kid—and now her best friend was gay. The conjecture ended when Anthony's brother, Francis, entered the picture.

They met while she was back in Los Angeles during a break from the tour. Natalie had already met most of Anthony's brothers—Walfredo, Michael, and the triplets, Giovanni, Giuseppe and Giorgio—but not Anthony's elusive brother Francis, the black sheep, who preferred to be called Frank. He was an inventor. He lived alone. He didn't come home to New Jersey for

Christmas. From what she'd heard, Natalie thought Anthony's brother Frank might be gay, too.

"My brother's in L.A. for some kind of exposition," Anthony said to Natalie when he called from New York one afternoon. "Will you take him around and show him the city? He's never been there before. Mama's worried about him getting into trouble."

"Sure," she said. "What's the number where he's staying? What does he like to do?"

"Who knows? All he does is read and study and fuss with what he's making. It's the Holiday Inn on Ventura Boulevard. Maybe don't take him to the bars, though."

She laughed. "I'll scratch that idea from the list. OK, I'll figure something out. How's your break?"

Anthony told her about a young man he'd met at a café in the Village. They were seeing one another and Anthony said he thought this time it might be serious. He talked about Pedro, a waiter who was studying at fashion school. Anthony thought he was adorable and it turned out that he was and the feeling was mutual.

"Natty, I think I'm in love."

"Have you slept with him?" She asked, folding some laundry.

"Not yet. But I want to. He's younger than me. I want to take things slow."

"So, it *is* serious. Oh my. Keep me posted."

"I will."

"Anthony?"

"Yes?"

"I'm happy for you." She said it softly, the way she talked when they'd first started hanging out. Anthony thanked her and said goodbye. As he hung up, he immediately wondered if she didn't sound a little left out and depressed. He rang his brother Francis at the hotel.

"Hello, this is Frank." His brother's voice was flat, dry and deep.

"Hey, it's Anthony."

"Hi, listen I can't talk long because I'm headed out for a demonstration at the expo. What's up?"

"I just wanted to let you know that I gave your hotel number to Natalie and she said she's looking forward to finally meeting you. Maybe she can take you around to the La Brea tar pits and museums and stuff like that."

"Yeah, yeah, you already told me, Anthony, and like I said that's fine. I want to meet your friend. No problem—anything else?"

His younger brother paused and there was a brief silence.

"Treat her well, Frank. I love Natalie and she deserves to have a brighter day. Don't shut her out. Let her in."

Something about the way his little brother said that made Frank take notice that little Anthony—"Squirt" to the rest of the Stefano boys—was all grown up. "Say," he said, "how's your new boyfriend?"

That took Anthony by surprise. "We're good."

"I want to meet him, too."

That was an even bigger surprise. They said goodbye and hung up, both sensing their bond was a bit deeper than it had been a few minutes ago.

Like his brother Anthony, Frank Stefano was aptly described as tall, dark and handsome, only he was thicker and slightly taller at 6 feet 2 inches, and he was darker, with more distinctly Sicilian features, and, with his broken nose, deep-set dark brown eyes and a heavier bush of black hair on his brow he could have passed for a mobster had he worn a Fedora and a striped suit— even in his trademark t-shirt and blue jeans. He looked like a brooding hulk that might have been a linebacker, a bouncer or a heavy for the mob. Frank Stefano was an inventor with patents pending in three different industries. He was used to people underestimating him.

It was love at first sight with Natalie Harris. She phoned the Holiday Inn and he thought she was room service calling back about his burger and fries. "Yeah, where's that cheeseburger?" he answered. "I don't know," she replied, amused by the contrast with her best friend. "But if I did, I would tell you." She paused. "Is this Francis Stefano?" "Yeah," he'd said. "Are you Anthony's buddy?" "Yes. About the cheeseburger. I can pick one up for you on the way over if you'd like."

He couldn't have been less interested in any activity than he was in following a female around L.A., especially when there was important business to mind at the expo. He'd made important new contacts here and had several investors interested in what he had to make and sell. The last thing he wanted to do was hang around one of his brother's snooty ballerinas.

"Nyahh, I'm waiting on some grub from room service—sorry about that. Can you be here by two? I've got a few hours to kill before I have to go back to work." He was brusque, which she didn't like about him. Not one bit.

"Fine," she sniffed, "Anthony said you needed showing around. I can see why. How about I take you to an automotive museum this afternoon? That seems like a place you might like."

"See you at two. Meet me in the lobby." He spoke like she was his assistant and it was 1951. But it was the early 1990s and Natalie didn't take to being talked to like that.

"Yes, sir," she said, ready to hang up—

"Your name's Natalie, right?"

"Yes, it is, Francis." She shot back.

"My name is Frank. Ma and my kid brother call me Francis. I don't know you, so call me Frank."

She forgot about that and felt sorry. But she chose not to say so. Then he said: "Also, I'll drive." And he hung up. She had known Anthony for years and had met his entire family, except this one brother. Flushing red at being hung up on, she decided on the spot that she hated Frank Stefano.

She felt no differently when she approached him in the lobby of the Holiday Inn—until their eyes met. He smoldered. She radiated. They both knew they were smitten.

"Hi." It was his voice, commanding yet gentle while he sized her up. Suddenly, everything on the phone made sense. "Hi." She said it with a hint of lust. She wanted him right then and there. Honestly, she would have been happy to have been taken on the spot had he indicated he was open to the idea. She could tell by the way he looked at her—like she was a piece of tender meat—that he wanted her. She could also tell that he relished the idea with a bit of a jaunty air. "You ready?" He asked. Natalie threw her head back and played right along.

"In a moment. Do you mind waiting for me?" She asked, her eyes searching the lobby. He nodded and watched her walk toward a lobby attendant and disappear into a hallway. He liked the way she moved when she walked. For the first time, he became aware that she was a dancer. When she returned, he saw that she had freshened up. Her hair was fuller, her lips were redder, her blouse had been loosened. He thought: so, she likes to be noticed.

She thought: so, he likes to notice me. There was an animal quality about him that she had observed, but it was the fact that he was in control of it that drew her in.

"Let's go," Frank said, turning away and barely extending his elbow as he did. She stepped forward and slipped her arm into his and they went out the double doors to his rental car.

There was something perpetually hungry about both Frank and Natalie. He was always eyeing her as an object for his personal pleasure, gazing upon her silently during dinner, and he was no less a sex object to her, and both of them were an embodiment of repressed sexual desire for the other. There was a forbidden air to their chemistry, too. But there was also a confidence about them—the overwhelming sense that everything would be fine, better, even terrific, between them. Not as though they had all the time in the world. But that they could have, if they wanted it.

Frank came to Los Angeles often in those days, for business meetings, sales pitches and scouting for startup locations. They met every time, just the two of them, and told no one of their affair, until Frank finally made Natalie his own in a tent they'd pitched during a picnic in Griffith Park near the observatory. He picked her up and set her down and had his way, making love for hours while she moaned with the erotic release of pent-up pleasure. At dusk, they laid outside on a blanket looking at the stars, holding hands and breathing quietly under the sun-streaked, barely twinkling sky. He figured now was the time to ask: "Will you marry me?" and he'd said it just like that. She thought for a few minutes and turned away, struggling with what her psychiatrist had warned her about with regard to early childhood trauma and how she felt in the moment. She rolled over and looked into Frank's saucer-like eyes of dark brown. "Yes," she breathed. Slowly, she lifted and wrapped one leg around his waist and pulled herself up on top of him, her hips in line with his.

By then, Natalie Harris was a reedy woman with bright eyes, a gay laugh and a tense, high-strung disposition. She had danced through life, waiting for a man worthy of her, and she was ready for love.

One night while she was performing in a ballet at the Dorothy Chandler Pavilion, she suddenly became keenly aware that someone was watching her…intently. There were a thousand pairs of eyes enjoying her performance. However, she felt a particular stare as though it had x-ray vision, piercing her soul. It was not a stalker's stare. This was more like a familiar stare, one that was not unlike an old friend or a protector. During a movement where she had a break from dancing and was on stage left, she started to scan the audience. She found her mark on a top balcony. But he wasn't anyone she could remember seeing. Curiously, she wondered if this wasn't a possible soul mate. Then she started wondering if she had made a hasty choice in Frank, if she shouldn't keep her options open. Should she pursue this person of interest after the performance? Surely many matrons and patrons from the balconies would come forward to congratulate performers. She could meet him then. If for no other reason than to find out more about him and his background.

Was she out of her mind? She had just accepted a marriage proposal from Frank, with whom she was in fact seriously in love. She pondered a moment, then shook it off as she almost missed her next cue. She had to wait until the end of the performance to see if this pair of eyes was backed up by a face and a name.

After the ballet ended, she was on stage and then backstage accepting the usual flowers, boxes of candy, etc. for another flawless performance. Alas, no one connected. Some elderly men looked at her as a trophy to take home for the night, but no one with a connection at a glance. This mysterious man had vanished. Natalie finally accepted that nothing special was going to happen and she headed for her dressing room, deciding it must have been her imagination or a fluke.

The wedding was planned for that summer, with Anthony as the best man, Patrice as the maid of honor, and of course Roy giving away the bride in a small, religious garden ceremony with a reception at the Sportsmen's Lodge. If it weren't for the stranger lurking at the edge of the garden, you'd never know that Natalie was marrying another man in another time.

But Roy, who had been beset by nightmares, the unsolved murder of his wife's late husband, and the nagging memory of suspicious posers such as Eleanor Jones, sensed something strange that day. Having received an anonymous gun had put him on edge. His daughter's wedding had him on guard. Spotting the stranger in a Fedora pacing back and forth near the edge of the garden, a short distance from the wedding, where string music had started to play, the police detective calculated that he had enough time to investigate.

Roy pursued the stranger, who briskly walked away, around a hedge corner. Roy followed him until he lost sight. He backtracked in another direction, finally meeting the stranger face to face by a pond and confronting the man who was my master, charge and surrogate son, Jeff Thurman. Jeff pulled his hat's brim downward, said he had made a mistake and apologized for the intrusion.

"I was lost in my thoughts and prayers," he told the policeman—the father of a bride who had once been his bride. "I stumbled into this wedding in error." His voice did not betray his emotions. Jeff managed to conceal his true feelings.

Roy felt the stranger's intensity and put his hand on the man's shoulder. "Let me help you find your way," he said to the time traveler.

"You already have," came the reply. In an instant, he'd stepped away and was gone. The first strains of the wedding march had already begun.

Chapter 10: Diary

I haven't much time to write this, so I'll hurry things up if you don't mind. I must say that, at this point, I knew that Jeff Thurman was deeply affected by his backdated act of vengeance—though the results had exceeded his most optimistic projections—and the wedding of the woman who had, once upon a time, been his bride and had taken her own life, induced the most important and agonizing choice in his young, complicated life.

High-strung Natalie would have something to say about his choice, too. First, let me tell you the rest of the story in its proper order. Jeff would have liked me to do that, I think, though I can't be sure and, with time running out, I honestly do not know whether I'll have the chance to ask him. The sun is setting and it seems like the sky is falling, but for me the end is a matter of time. Back to the tale.

At the end of the 20th century, almost everything was coming together for Det. Roy Harris. His wife enjoyed her life and newfound work, his happy marriage got a boost from having an almost empty nest—with mutual parental knowledge of a job well done—and more time for one another. His son Mike was serving with his wife Patrice in the U.S. Navy, and his grandson Rodger was recognized for his academic excellence at Cal Tech. His moody daughter Natalie had met and married inventor Frank Stefano, whom she'd met through her best friend Anthony, who was now living with his partner, Pedro. Even Roy's partner and best friend, Earl, still on the force and moonlighting as a security consultant for an electrical utility, was happy. Earl took them sailing every other Sunday in the *Whalewatcher*.

The two off-duty cops were moving with full sail hoisted and whipping in the crosswinds off Catalina Island when Earl called out across the way over the noise of the boat and the whooshing of the waves: "Still bothered by the Warner murder?"

Roy was on the brink of his 65th birthday and taking an honest estimate of his life. He'd made an important decision earlier in the year on the occasion of Natalie's wedding day.

"That's in the past," he called back to his friend, a new lightness in his voice that caught even him by surprise. "I'm letting it go." Just then a gust swept the *Whalewatcher*, tilting her to starboard until the men righted her with ropes and sails. The two detectives, who had worked together as partners for over 40 years, toiled wordlessly in the blazing sun, wind and spray from the whitecaps, tossing back an occasional beer and nodding back and forth as warranted while gliding past the island at 30 knots. *This is it*, Roy thought as he pulled ropes, loosened others and generally let the *Whalewatcher* rip, pausing to survey the horizon—where the sun-kissed ocean met the clear blue sky—and feeling on top of the world. *Life is rich. I'm happy in my skin. It doesn't get better than this.*

Maybe not, but it would get worse, and sooner than Roy thought. This leads me to tell you about Roy's grandson—Mike and Patrice's offspring—Rodger, an incorrigible, skinny lad with tousled hair who was hell-bent on making his way in the world. He would prove crucial in what was to happen next.

"I want to go ahead in time," Rodger wrote boldly in his diary when he was eleven. "My family's been stuck in the past and present and I love them, but I have no patience for either–let me get to the future and get me out of this lousy century." The kid wrote like an adult. And he meant what he wrote.

Here's more, from when he was 16:

"*I'm convinced that something happened to my Aunt Natalie, but nobody talks about it. I sense something disturbing—can't quite identify it—and it's there, dogging her, driving her in some way toward excellence or doom. I don't know it for certain. I haven't had any clues or evidence. Just a sense that something's off. I don't understand why—yet. Whatever it is must be terrible.*"

Rodger's diary was a log of scientific theories, reports, studies and lessons in school, and, later, college and graduate school. Yet Rodger was always a keen and diligent observer of Harris family life, too. While in college, he noted:

"*Today we went sailing again. Earl hasn't had me out on the Whalewatcher in months. With all the lab work I've been doing it was good to get out in the open again. The old snipe's seen better days, but this time we went with Grandpa Roy and Dad and the four of us had the best day yet. We sailed north to Santa Barbara, past the Channel Islands, toward Morro Bay, and we charted every seal, whale, shark and fish we could find...*"

"*Grandpa's a case, that's for sure. He's happy about his life and he's had an amazing life. After we anchored at sea and sat back for some grilled salmon, we listened to Grandpa talk about himself while he carved. He went from beat cop to homicide detective within a few years and he's put some of the worst killers away for good. He replaced someone, everyone says, who was a great statesman when he married Grandma. He raised my dad and Aunt Natty and, so far as I can tell, there's not a better man who takes pride in his work and his family and loves them for who they are— a real man, not just another old man. My grandfather is modern, but he is moral and decent and good. I think I got my sense of justice from him.*"

"Yet even Grandpa is haunted by the past. I know he and my dad can go for hours talking about homicide, especially the unsolved murder of Grandma's first husband, the one they talk about most. Grandpa mentioned an eyewitness report of a stranger near the murder scene, which Dad thinks may be connected to the homicide—but Earl mocks that report, which he says came from an old lady with seven cats, impaired vision and a '52 Studebaker in the driveway, that Earl says looks like a bug-eyed beast with two fangs and a few teeth missing. Whoever murdered my father's father hasn't heard the last of Grandpa Roy. He'll get him, if there is a him to get. I know he will."

A few months later, Rodger wrote about Thanksgiving at the grandparents:

"We watched sports and Uncle Frank and I played video games. He's an interesting guy. Different, not like Dad and Grandpa or Earl. More reserved. When I asked about his latest projects, Uncle Frank told me he's not ready to talk about it yet. He's been saying that ever since I can remember. Something about the way he talks in that New Jersey accent makes me think he'll make good on whatever he's invented. Maybe not now or tomorrow or even next year. Maybe in five years or ten. We competed on Battlemaster for an hour and he was telling me about spatial relationships and the dynamics of certain things with certain properties that interact and still he beat me every time. Uncle Frank knows a lot about a lot of things and he puts his ideas into action. He reminds me of Dr. Manther."

Rodger went on and on about his graduate studies, classes and professors in his diary, for pages on end. Then he returned to his thoughts on Thanksgiving.

"Grandma said a prayer and then led a toast before Thanksgiving dinner, thanking Mom and Dad for their military service, Aunt Natty and Uncle Frank for their inspiration and innovation and Grandpa for what she called his exceptional career in law enforcement. Then she looked at me and said she was thankful that I hadn't had my nose pierced and everyone laughed. Little does she know I've tattooed my treasure trail with an American eagle and I'm thinking of piercing my ears. No one but a couple of friends and Professor Manther knows about the tattoo."

"This is my first Thanksgiving with Mom and Dad since I lived at home in San Diego. They're scheduled to go back to sea in a few days and then I won't see them for months as usual. But I read their letters and I know they read mine and if it weren't for their service in the Navy and my living with my grandparents during college and grad school, I doubt I'd be keeping this diary. I do love my parents and I know I have a good life. But sometimes—OK, oftentimes—I want to ditch the past and depart the present and leap into the future to see what's gone wrong and what's gone right and make sure that what happens matches what ought to happen. I have a sense that that's not always the case. And it ought to be."

Rodger Harris, if you haven't already observed, was a bundle of energy, enthusiasm and brains inside a tall, thin rail of toned, young muscle. He had bronzed skin under an unruly mop of auburn hair just like his mother's. Go near his room at Roy and Arlene's house and you'd hear hard rock or hip-hop or country at full volume and more than once his grandmother could be heard by neighbors screaming: "Rodger Harris, turn that blasted music down!!!" He wore Black Sabbath t-shirts as easily as he wore tight designer suits he'd picked up from second-hand shops on Melrose where he hung out with his artist friends. He went to swing dancing nights on Sunset Boulevard and lectures on thermonuclear dynamics, screenwriting and ethics; and he understood what he heard and often wrote about it in his diary, or, later, on his blog.

Rodger Harris was more of an academic athlete than merely a bright student, always sitting in the front row. And always the first on his feet after class to ask the instructor a question. His grades were exemplary and he was invited to attend Cal Tech to major in physics and mathematics on a private scholarship from an anonymous benefactor.

In his third year of grad school, Rodger became interested in a controversial Cal Tech guest lecturer whom he'd met through his physics professor. The speaker had talked about the past, present and future with radical theories on space and time and Rodger wanted to know more, so he attended the lecture series. After a lengthy and technical presentation, the speaker, Dr. F.J. Manther, listened to the wild-eyed student. He observed that beneath that nest of hair that concealed his eyes and face, the student had asked a good if not misguided question. Answering coolly: "It's not exactly that visiting the future is possible," the grizzled older teacher said, "but that taking corrective action to the past may prove practical—and, to some, irresistible." With that, young Rodger was at once speechless and spellbound.

"Here," the old man said, slipping a card into Rodger's palm, "call my office on Thursday to schedule a visit and I shall further illuminate the subject at hand." At that, Dr. F.J. Manther disappeared into a throng of students and faculty filing out of the lecture hall.

A more recent entry in Rodger's diary turned into a shocking report with serious consequences. It was dated shortly after his grandfather's 65th birthday, when Roy had decided to retire. He had finally shed the troubling thoughts about never solving the case of his wife's deceased husband's murder. Then, the press caught wind of the heroic cop's retirement and a new round of reports surfaced, only this time with new information. Rodger wrote:

> *"It started out as a perfectly fine day and it got worse. I had another amazing conversation with Dr. Manther after class about my thesis. I was thrilled that he offered me an apprenticeship at his lab out near where my dad used to live as a kid in Pasadena. Dr. Manther said it might even turn into a job when I get my Ph.D. if he can get the grant funded. So, I'm heading home on the freeway thinking of what I'm going to tell Mom and Dad in my next letter when I drive up and see the street blocked off by police barricades. Driving past Grandpa and Grandma's house, I turned and saw a cluster of police cars, cameras and microphones in front of the house. My gut churned and I parked in the first spot I saw and ran to the house as fast as I could.*

"I spotted Grandma as soon as I came upon the house. She was standing in the middle of the lawn in a pair of slacks and a windbreaker, calmly talking to a reporter with a microphone while a cameraman filmed the interview. Our eyes met, but before I knew it, a policeman herded me into the house, muttering something about new developments in some case Grandpa Roy had worked on a long time ago. I kept demanding to know where Grandpa was and the officer pointed to the study. He left me there in the hallway by my bedroom—my dad's old room—and I turned to see my grandmother still being interviewed, while a bunch of policemen stood on guard over the property."

"The house seemed eerily quiet, so I braced myself and felt my stomach spinning with bewilderment at what might have happened. Had one of Grandpa Roy's cases gone bad? Tossed out of court? Had someone escaped prison—hey, I know it happens—or been exonerated? I hesitated until I heard a news helicopter overhead. Knowing that Grandpa heard it, too, I entered. My grandfather, this great man who had just finished his police career and had been happy in life, was up against something. I knew I had to go to him and offer my support."

"I went into the study, which was darkened by closed shutters but for a single sunbeam of late-day light. I saw him sitting in his leather office chair. He was calm, he was still, and it seemed like he was simmering in anger. I decided to make my presence known."

"Grandpa?" I think I sounded like I was three years old—I felt that small again. He looked up without haste, noticing me, marking me for identification outside of his closely held inner context, and slowly he moaned recognition. "Mmm." It was all I heard. "Are you OK?" I asked the question because he looked as though he'd seen a ghost—an evil spirit. Something demonic. My mind was reeling now. I started making instant internal connections and, just then, I heard the front door close and the sound of Grandma

Arlene's voice.

"Rodger?"

"In here, Grandma."

"Ah, there you are. I'm glad you're home. Now, there's been some fuss, and I don't want you involved. We're all fine here, so I want you to go to one of your friends' houses—don't let the press follow you, so go out dressed in a disguise and let the policemen take you to your car—and stay there until we call."

"Are you and Grandpa in any danger?" I asked, now terribly concerned.

She smiled. "Not anymore, dear. What happened was a long time ago, and it's all over, but it's very unpleasant and I want you to know it's all over now. You're going to hear about it later, but your granddad is in the middle of this and so he needs some space and time to think things over."

I nodded, wondering what the heck had happened.

"This has nothing to do with you," she said, turning solemn for a moment and holding my shoulders. "I want you to know that I know you're a man and you can handle what's happened. But not right now, dear. Not now. Do you understand?"

"Yes, Grandma."

"Now off you go. I've packed some sandwiches and lemonade for you. They're in a cooler in the fridge. Go on, Rodger. I'll call you later."

"Yes, Grandma."

I went to leave and made it halfway to the door, but I couldn't resist one last look at my grandpa. His face was all knotted up in emotion.

"Go ahead," she repeated. "Earl's on his way here and everything's fine." She thought of one more thing. "Rodger, you're going to hear and read things. Just remember that we didn't know everything. Some of it we did—well, I did—and most of it we didn't. Try not to

blame us." On the last two words, her voice cracked and, for the first time, I saw that she was barely holding herself together. Grandma Arlene was trying to be strong. Something terrible had come undone—was it the something terrible I'd guessed at when I was a teenager? and my grandma was buckling under the strain. I threw my arms around her and held her close. I felt her silently collapse. We were like that for minutes until Grandpa spoke from behind the wooden desk. "Go on, son." He said and his voice was firm. "Do as your grandmother said."

Wearing a hooded sweatshirt, baseball cap and sunglasses, carrying a cooler and my backpack and with two cops on either side, I went to my car unnoticed. I searched in my mind for which friend to call upon— Marie, Tim, Sal, Sandy or Leroy—and decided to call someone I trusted with my life. I reached for something in my pocket, found what I was looking for, and placed the call from my mobile phone.

"Dr. Manther," came the answer.

There Rodger's diary entry had ended. The rest of the day was a blank. There hadn't been much more to say after that. It couldn't have been easy for the youngster, who must have learned one way or another what all of the world had learned earlier in the day: that, in reviewing the career of retiring detective, Roy Harris, the unsolved case of Senator James Warner's murder in 1959 had been revisited as well, and a top news Website reported in an exclusive report that Senator Warner had been involved in a children's sex trafficking ring with the heiress Eleanor Jones and several others. Jones had been arrested at her Bel-Air estate that afternoon. The news cast the late, supposedly great senator's murder in a whole new light. Frank and Natalie Stefano were traveling in Hong Kong when the news broke and Rodger's parents were safely at sea on a nuclear submarine.

Jeff Thurman, I knew, had prevented and avenged. But he had not been able to purge the past entirely of injustice.

Chapter 11: Angels

Roy Harris held the gun in his hand, turning it slowly and examining it. A fine weapon, he thought upon inspection. Not unlike the police department-issued semi-automatic handgun he'd used on the force during most of his career. Someone had sent him this fully loaded piece and, now that the homicide case on which he had worked for most of his life had a devastating new development (which he and Earl had not detected), Roy wondered if someone wasn't trying to send him a message.

Roy felt guilty. He had let Eleanor Jones slip away with a child sex trafficking ring and he couldn't stop thinking about how many kids had lost their lives and innocence. His mind was swirling with thoughts about leads, interviews and reports in decades-old case files for Senator Warner's murder. Had Eleanor Jones murdered the senator? One of the abused kids' parents? Someone involved in the trafficking? What to make of those eyewitness reports of a stranger, an explosion and the mysterious lights?

He'd gone over his notes on T.K. Chase and Eleanor Jones and their affiliation with Warner's campaign and senatorial duties and he'd read the transcript of his and Earl's 1960 interview with Mrs. Jones again and again. Just now, he could hear Earl's voice in the kitchen, where he was talking with Arlene. They'd both been walking on eggshells since the news broke, and media crews had only grown larger in size outside his home, adding to the tension. *Terrible New Twist in Retired Cop's Unsolved Case*, was the screaming Internet headline on one site. The sub headline was worse: *Murdered Senator Named in Child Sex Scandal.*

At least the kids were safe with their spouses—Mike was underwater somewhere in the Pacific and Natalie was in Hong Kong—and his grandson was safe with one of his college professors. Now it was only him and the two people with whom he had carried this homicide burden for nearly half a century: his police partner and his marital partner, both of whom had been at the scene of the crime on the night James Warner was shot to death.

Roy set the firearm down on the desk in front of him and sat back in his office chair. He'd been sitting in the study thinking in silence, coming to bed long after midnight every night since the arrest. That gun was a crucial clue, he thought. Someone knew something. Someone knew who killed Senator Warner. Someone wanted to let him in on it. But someone was hiding and that could mean he or she or their agents posed a danger to him and his family.

His family. The thought had been there all along. He had felt like he'd rescued this young family in 1959 when he took the beautiful, young widow and her kids to Disneyland, courting her and proposing marriage. He figured he'd set things right—or set things for the traumatized Warner family on the right track toward a better life. Roy had loved Mike and Natalie as his own children. Arlene was his soulmate, his friend, his wife. Now he found himself wondering what she knew and when she knew it—and what, if anything, had happened to the kids. Had Mike and Natalie been hurt by their father or Eleanor Jones or their cohorts? Had the kids repressed any memory? Had Arlene known? Was it conceivable that she might *not* have known? Roy knew after decades of working on these types of domestic abuse and homicide cases that the wives were not passive bystanders when fathers abused children—they were sometimes aware of the abuse, sometimes in on the action, and often they suspected something was wrong or had witnessed the abuse and did nothing. When he'd looked into his wife's eyes after hanging up with the police chief, who had just informed him about Eleanor Jones' arrest, he saw the jolt of shock on her face, then a concern for him, then, in her eyes after she drew a breath, he saw what he was sure was a hint of guilt, as if she knew something and suddenly became aware of its implications.

Roy Harris stared at the gun lying on his desk. It was a physical artifact that proved people—maybe people close to him—knew crucial things about a murder that was his job to solve, which had consumed his career and shaped his life. He was steaming with anger, stinging with guilt and above all he was coping with what he felt as a deep sense of betrayal. He was trying to sort things out, but the mind was flooded and the emotions were spinning. So, for now, hearing hushed tones from his wife and partner in the kitchen, he sat back and he thought—and he thought some more. *I must think through this*, he thought. He was fixated on the gun.

Down the hall, past the living room, where, except for slits, shutters were closed to shield the occupants from blinding yellowish-white floodlights for live shots from television cameras on the front lawn, Earl and Arlene spoke in whispers in the Harris family kitchen.

"We've got to get him out of there," Earl said gazing down the hallway. "I know he's reeling and rehashing and that can only lead to trouble."

Arlene sat on the counter stool, dressed in shorts and a short-sleeved, white knit top with stripes of light blue. She looked rested and athletic. Calm and in command, typing notes and e-mails on her laptop computer on the kitchen counter, a cup of black coffee within reach. "Earl, he's fine in there," she said plainly. "He's figuring things out. Let him be."

"I don't think he's fine, Arlene," Earl confided.

She came right back. "Of course he isn't fine. I didn't say he was. I said he's fine *in there*. I suggest that you leave him be."

Arlene took it down a notch. "It's you who isn't fine, and especially not in here. You need to be out on the open sea or in there with your partner." At that, she stopped what she was doing on the computer and looked over at him, standing with his arms folded and his back against the counter by the kitchen sink. Her expression turned to sympathy.

"Look, I know this is huge," she admitted. "I'm not saying it isn't. I can't pretend to know what you two are going through, having missed this crime. The time will come for me to sort through all this with Roy and the kids. Right now, he needs to cool off and think. You need to take care of yourself and tend to your own feelings about Jim's murder and the Eleanor Jones arrest and what those two were doing to children. Go in there and tell my husband you need to vent."

There was a long pause. Earl looked at Arlene for a long time. It was a cross between a scowl and a pout.

"I need to vent something to you," he said, keeping his voice low.

She looked at him. Square in the eye. His eyes were wet. She'd known Earl for most of her life—he was the one who took her by the hand on the night she broke through the police lines and saw her husband's lifeless body and it was Earl who escorted her to the police station. He had been the one to explain why she had to be questioned and considered as a prime suspect. Earl had been a good friend to her family. She wanted to know what was on his mind. She was afraid to hear it.

"OK," she said, turning to him.

"I want to know what happened to you and the kids before Warner was murdered," he said evenly. "You've never talked about what it was like to be a senator's wife and I know that was a long time ago. But I need to know what happened." She could see that this wasn't easy for Earl to say. "I think Roy deserves to know, too."

After a minute, she said, "You're right, Earl." Then she added: "In time. I'll tell you in time."

Her friend inclined his head. "I can live with that, Arlene." He said, moving toward the hallway, "and I think you may be right about the need to talk to our buddy." As he exited the kitchen, Earl stopped and turned his head. "Thank you," he said. Arlene watched him disappear into the darkness toward Roy's study.

She turned back to her computer. The e-mail exchanges between Arlene and her children had been short and pointed.

Something's happened here and your father's feeling down, she wrote to Mike's Navy e-mail address. *Will keep you posted.*

Is Dad OK? Mike wrote back.

Yes. More later, son. Rodger's staying with Dr. Manther til this blows over.

OK. Thanks Mom.

Then, a few hours later, from Mike: *Does he know?*

Arlene's reply: *Not yet. Soon, Mike. He needs space. He needs time.*

Mike: *Does Natalie know something's happened?*

In fact, Arlene had sent the same notification she'd sent to Mike to her daughter, who was on vacation with Frank in Hong Kong while Frank was meeting various businessmen, dealers and manufacturers to arrange the manufacture and distribution of one of his pending inventions.

Natalie had responded with a one-line message: *Mom, I'm coming home.*

Home was splintered, as far as Arlene Warner Harris was concerned. She had postponed reliving the past, and the arrest of Eleanor Jones brought it roaring back, increasing the risk of springing leaks all over. A routine traffic violation led to a flagged arrest record that led to a missing child that led to someone who claimed he'd been hired by Eleanor Jones and that's when the whole thing blew wide open. Now, the worldwide media was camped out on Arlene's front lawn, with cops surrounding the Harris residence and rallying to Roy's defense. City leaders and church, community and charity types were on the side of sweet, old Eleanor Jones, whom they had coddled for four decades.

Roy was in solitude, hurt and angry and not saying much to his wife. Mike was worried about the man who'd raised him. Natalie was on edge—possibly snapping into jeopardy. Rodger was in the dark about all of this, or so his grandmother thought. And elderly, wispy Eleanor Jones was in the custody of the Los Angeles Police, where Arlene was driving to right now— a scarf loosely wrapped around her head and tied under her chin and wearing a pair of sunglasses—to see her dead husband's accomplice and partner in crime…

Earl didn't bother to knock. He strode down the hallway and crossed the threshold into Roy's study and the first thing he saw was a gun lying on the desk in front of his former partner.

"You want to explain that?" He asked, looking at the weapon.

"It's a gun," Roy, slumped in his office chair, said. "You ought to try firing one sometime. You might actually hit something."

"Come on, Roy. That's not yours. Whose is it? And what are you doing with it?"

Roy leaned back and thought for a moment. "It was an anonymous gift. I'm studying it."

Earl was more intrigued than concerned. "Was there a note?"

"Yes. Said it was from a friend," Roy looked up at Earl and smirked. "Is it from you?"

But Earl was staring at it intently—a stern expression on his face. "No. And for all you know it might be connected to the Warner case."

"After today, I think half of Los Angeles might be connected to the Warner case," Roy replied, referring to the sex ring. "I don't know what to think anymore."

Earl parked himself on the edge of Roy's desk and sighed. "This is brutal, chief. I know it. It was a long time ago and we did what we could. We didn't have DNA and ballistics back then like we do now. This killer was a pro. Now we know that when he shot Senator Warner, he didn't kill a Boy Scout. I stood by you when you married Arlene, and we both know you took some heat for that, and I'll stand by you now. We've been through a lot on this case. Eleanor Jones will probably get what she deserves." Earl looked over his shoulder and lowered his voice. "I know he was your kids' dad, Roy, but maybe the senator got what he deserved, too."

Roy shot him a glance. "How did we miss this?"

"How did we miss a lot of things? You'll go nuts asking those questions. How can we fix it now? That's the only question that counts. We have to have your gift tested for prints and ballistics. This may be the break we need. Not what we would have wanted, not at all, but it is what it is and now we have to deal with it. That's what you always taught me." Earl reached over and nudged Roy, who was still in his slump. "Partner."

Earl changed the subject. "Listen, Arlene took off somewhere and I have to go to my utility job. But I don't like leaving you here alone, especially with that gun."

"I'm fine. Where are you headed?"

"I'm off to a location for the power company," Earl said.

"Oh, that's right. How's it going?"

"Eh." He shrugged. "It's not like working homicide. Boring stuff mostly. Kids spraying graffiti on walls, stuff like that. Basic security. There's been another report of a power theft—at a power station near the old Warner murder scene as a matter of fact—so I have to check it out." Earl looked down at his dejected, retired, worn-out partner, who'd been hiding from the world and was now staring at a gun. "So," he added: "Wanna come along?"

Roy couldn't get up fast enough.

With that, the entire Harris family was in turmoil and in transit. Roy was by his partner's side again on a security job to investigate a power theft in Pasadena. Arlene was off to Parker Center downtown to meet her murdered husband's criminal partner in jail. Natalie had kissed Frank goodbye in Hong Kong and was on a passenger jet over the Pacific Ocean—just 150 miles from and 30,000 feet above where her brother Mike was cruising with Patrice in a nuclear submarine, studying certain issues with earthquakes, oceanic activity, black holes, solar flares and the position of the sun. Only Rodger remained stationary. He was engrossed in monitoring an instrumental adjustment on one of the experimental measurement machines in a Pasadena laboratory near NASA at the home of his friend, mentor and tutor, Dr. F.J. Manther.

He was trying to not think of his family's crisis. Dr. Manther, a befuddled, disheveled man whom Rodger guessed to be younger than he appeared, had noticed his demeanor when Rodger showed up for work at the lab.

"Everything OK?" The professor had asked upon his arrival.

"No, but it probably will be," Rodger had answered, being characteristically scientific. "My grandmother sent me out and told me to stay with a friend for a few days. Thanks for letting me stay here while I'm working."

"Not a problem," the academic replied, "not a problem at all. There are some extra blankets in the guest room closet. Help yourself in the kitchen as usual."

"Thanks, Dr. Manther. What's to be done?"

With that, the stuttering genius had provided him with an endless list of tasks and duties and there they were, at well past midnight, tuning and adapting and testing in the basement lab while Rodger's grandfather and Earl drove unknowingly past the dark, low-slung Pasadena ranch house.

The house was tucked into the hills surrounding the Rose Bowl a few blocks from the house where Senator Warner had been murdered. The white mid-century modern structure looked clean and simple in the daytime, set far back from the street on a deep, wide property with oranges, lemons and over a hundred trees extending far back to another hill, beyond which a Los Angeles County power station occupied a few acres.

Dr. Manther had lived there near Cal Tech and NASA's Jet Propulsion Laboratory for years and he'd made a lab in the basement for his own studies and experiments. A driveway curved at the front of the house, sloping down the hill into the street, which contained several other houses on large estates.

At nighttime, a single light glowed from the front of the Manther house, softly illuminating the front door. The modern house on the unlighted Wichita Lane was barely visible from the street after sundown, sitting high above the street in darkness. Surrounded by hills, you could barely make out the roofline. Seen from street level, Dr. Manther's house looked like a mushroom with an angular roof on top.

Earl drove past the house as Roy looked on while they headed to the power station, not knowing that Rodger was inside working with Dr. Manther in a subterranean lab.

Roy and Earl pulled up to the power station security gate and Earl got out to unlock the gate. When they drove into the restricted area, Roy noticed no outward signs of a security breach.

"Lately, this substation gets hit all the time," Earl explained. "We've noticed high-voltage spikes during low-use times. I've tracked the power to a Cal Tech facility that's being routed to a residence on the other side of the hill but—"

"Earl, do you know where we are?" Roy blurted out.

"Yes."

"This is near the old Warner house."

"I know that."

Roy sighed. "Those poor kids ..." He trailed off. Earl looked at his lifelong friend in sympathy and put his hand on Roy's shoulder. Just then, Roy remembered something about that night in 1959.

"Earl, when we visited this transformer the night of the murder, did it have the security lock?"

"Not back then, no. Why?"

"How long have the thefts been reported by Southern California Edison?"

"Since a couple of weeks ago. I'm not following you though. Are we talking about the thefts or the murder?"

Roy looked out at the dark. "I don't know."

They got out of Earl's car, scoped the facility and walked around the power station. Nothing out of the ordinary. All systems were operational. But Earl's reports indicated that power was being drained and traced to Cal Tech and re-routed to a residential area. Recurrent high-voltage fluctuations were unusual during such low-power use times as after midnight.

They looked at the map, which crinkled in the night's wind. Roy pointed to a spot and made a circle with his finger. "Let's go," Earl said.

They drove to the spot on the map and parked at the end of a cul-de-sac overlooking the Rose Bowl and, in the distance, the city of Los Angeles. The night was as black as ink. "You take the south side of the street, Earl, I'll take the north," Roy said, as he closed the car door and crossed the street. They surreptitiously began to canvass the neighborhood for signs of unusual power use. As they did, with one on each side of the street, Roy's eyes widened as he approached a modern white house high up on a hill. There, in the curved driveway, was a car he recognized—it was his grandson's sedan. He reached into his pocket, pulled out his cellular phone and placed a call.

"H-h-hello—Grandpa?" It was Rodger's hesitant voice.

"Rodger, what's your location right now?"

"Grandpa, is that you?" Rodger answered, turning away from Dr. Manther for a moment during the surge of another experiment on the diagnostic machine in the basement. He could barely hear over the noise of machines, and he wondered why Grandpa Roy was calling at this hour. "Is everything OK?"

"Rodger, where are you?"

"I told Grandma. I'm with Dr. Manther."

"Come to the front door, son."

"Why? Are—where are you, Grandpa?"

"I'm standing on the pavement looking at your car."

"I'll be right out." Rodger, speaking above the steady drone of a machine in the basement corner, explained to Dr. Manther the unexpected intrusion and excused himself from his work. Dr. Manther, engaged in his latest project, nodded and took the information in stride. He told the young apprentice to welcome the visitor and bring him downstairs into the lab.

Standing at the top of Dr. Manther's driveway, Roy waved to Earl down on the other side of the street and pointed to Rodger's car, then to the house. Earl waved back and kept on canvassing. When Roy saw his grandson appear under the lone light at the front door, he walked over.

"Come in, Grandpa," Rodger greeted him. "Are you OK?"

"I'm fine," Roy replied, stepping inside. "I'm helping Earl on his power company job and I saw your car."

"Follow me. Dr. Manther wants us to come downstairs—we're in the middle of a diagnosis. You can meet my mentor!"

"Fine, Rodge, but I can't stay long. Tell me about the work you're doing here."

Rodger went on about the experiments and notations as they walked through the house, and, as he did, Roy noticed that it was plain and empty, except for a few pieces of furniture; but as they neared the staircase to the basement—a rare feature for a house in Southern California—he heard the whir and hum of a motor. It was low and steady. Roy went first as they descended into the lab.

The walls down there were composed of wooden beams and some substance Roy hadn't seen before; a lighter material of some type, he figured. Whatever it was, it blunted and contained the sound of the machine that was running. The cellar was an active center with wires, lights, motors and machines. Roy saw the back of a man standing over a drafting table and he heard him say: "Rodger, please go into the op center and access the intra-system. Please run the G program at full power."

"Yes, sir," came the reply, and, in a flash, Roy saw Rodger disappear around a corner.

Roy stood there for a moment, examining the activity around him. He started to say something when the professor turned around and extended his hand. "Nice to meet you, Mr. Harris."

He said it easily, as though meeting an old friend, and Roy said, "Nice to meet you, too. Some place you've got here." He looked at the doctor. Something about him felt familiar.

"Welcome. It's an honor to have you here," he said gravely.

"Do I know you?" Roy asked, and, as soon as he said it, he knew the answer. He caught his breath for a moment, stepped back and instantly groped inside his jacket for his holster. He knew it was the man he'd seen at Natalie's wedding. The stranger in the Fedora. But, this was Rodger's teacher—who?—how?—his mind was racing with a flurry of thoughts.

"Please," Dr. Manther said coolly, gesturing toward a leather office chair, "have a seat."

So he did. He kept his hand ready, but Roy seated himself. "Who are you?" He heard himself asking Dr. Manther.

"I expected it would be sooner rather than later when you came around to that question. I am your daughter's avenger."

At that, Roy's first response was protectiveness—so he yelled: "Rodger!!"

"There is no need to yell, Detective. He is in no danger. Besides, he can't hear you where he is," said the man calmly. "Neither can your ex-partner. Your communications are powerless in here." He added: "So is your weapon."

Roy reached for his gun and pulled it out, pointing at the stranger his son knew as Dr. Manther. "Get back," he said.

"That will not work here, Mr. Harris, but please. Grant me the benefit of the doubt. I intend you no harm. Quite the opposite."

Roy sized him up. "Start talking," he said. "Say what you've got on your mind before I blow a hole in your kneecap."

Jeff Thurman smiled. "Thank you, Mr. Harris."

He continued: "You are like the father I never had. You were there for your kids. You held them, you encouraged them. You guided them, you protected them, and you lived the example of being your best. You love your children. That made all the difference. I respect you, Mr. Harris."

Roy glared at him. He went on.

"I had to kill Senator Warner to change the children's lives. He had done terrible things to Mike and Natalie, and others, and he would have done worse—much worse—and he would have let others hurt them, too. I know you must know that, too, now that you know about Eleanor Jones."

"You see," he continued, "I come from another time, strange as that may sound. It has taken an effort to get here to do the deed, to stop James Warner. But he's dead. I killed him. It is something I wanted to do. Something I had to do."

All that Roy heard was that Senator Warner's killer had just confessed and he wanted to shove the gun in the guy's neck, get him handcuffed and get him to Parker Center. Not much else he said made sense—how could he have known what he claimed to know and what was this about time and respect?—but Warner's murderer stood before him. Still, Roy had the gun, and it was loaded and cocked, so he listened. "Go on," he said.

"I come from another time, Mr. Harris," he said evenly. "I traveled through time using a cruder version of that machine over there in the corner."

Roy glanced over and saw that it was running, a light flashing on a console and a motor making a droning sound.

"In my time," the stranger who was Jeff Thurman explained, "Senator Warner lived. His daughter Natalie did not. She was so damaged by what he'd done to her, that she took her own life. You see, Mr. Harris, Natalie Warner was my wife. I stand before you as her widower. I came back to change that fact. That's why I was there on her wedding day. To see for myself that I'd made good on my commitment to myself."

Roy did not believe what he heard. But he listened.

"In my time, Mike was a wreck," Jeff explained. "He was also damaged by what Senator Warner had done. I know this is hard to hear as their father, Mr. Harris. But your wife, Mrs. Harris, Arlene, she wasn't as nice or as innocent either, in my time. Everything had to change in order to make things right."

Roy's blood was rushing now. This man was talking about his wife.

"I was distraught about what had happened to my wife, to Natalie, and I decided to do something about it. I built a temporal dilation machine and I took the gun with which Natalie had killed herself, and I brought it back here to kill the man who had killed the love of my life. Natalie had found the gun at her father's house, in my time—it had belonged to Eleanor Jones, who left it at Senator Warner's house during one of her visits to the Warner household—and she used it to kill herself. When I came here to your time, Mr. Harris, I used it. After a time, I sent it to you, as a gift."

Roy was thinking of the Warner murder case files—witness reports of bursts of light and explosions and a stranger seen in the area. He listened.

Roy sat and stared at the stranger. Finally, he spoke. "Executioner," he said to the man, whose name he did not know—except that he knew it wasn't Manther as he'd been led to believe. "You are an executioner."

"I respect your conclusion, Mr. Harris," said the man. "Time will tell whether that's true. You may judge me for my actions. You may be right. Some will say I am an executioner, as you claim. Others may say I'm an avenger, as I claim. If you pull the trigger, that makes you an executioner, too. If you don't, by my reasoning, that makes you an avenger like me."

He paused.

"Even so, Mr. Harris, your gun won't work down here."

"I could arrest you for the murder of Senator James Warner," Roy said.

"You could", Jeff said. "Except for a couple of problems you would encounter in doing so. For one thing, your fingerprints are on it, not mine. And you would have to describe how a person born in 1959 was able to pull off a murder the same year. Also, you can't prove I gave it to you. You have been in possession of it for years. You were working in the San Fernando Valley when the senator was murdered. Who's to say you didn't do it to get access to his lovely wife?"

Roy spoke. "So, you think you've pulled off the perfect murder, do you? Got it all wrapped up in a bow? And made me the patsy of your plot?"

"No." Jeff said carefully. "The perfect murder is where I would end up with what I wanted, what I sought, in exchange for the death or deaths of others. This is not the case. I avenged our mutual family. I avenged Natalie. I altered time for good. But I did not end up with her. That … would have been the perfect murder. I take comfort in the fact that she is better off, that she has a brighter future. I cannot love her and have her as my wife, though. There is nothing, where once I had everything. Her happiness is my reward."

"I never intended to make you the fall guy. I needed insurance in case I was found out at some point so I didn't end up going to jail."

Roy had listened to what the stranger said. He processed his thoughts. Then he spoke.

"I have spent my whole career making sure that justice was done. That meant either someone going to prison, or someone going to the grave. Either way, someone is held accountable. I can't just walk away knowing who the shooter is."

"Justice is served," Jeff said, "And someone did go to the grave. But the guilty man is the one who died."

"Here's what you're going to do," Jeff went on. "You're going to deliver the new evidence, which your ex-partner Earl will claim he found on the old Warner estate property while doing routine patrols tonight. He'll bring the weapon to the police and report it as the murder weapon, implicating Eleanor Jones, the registered owner of the gun, as the murderer of Senator Warner. The case will be closed and that monster Jones will get what she deserves. But, first, you're going to go home with your grandson and think about what I've said and make your own judgment. I think you'll make the best choice."

"I can't just let you leave here," Roy said.

Just then, he heard another voice, not the man's and not his own—

"Please, Grandpa."

The voice was Rodger's. Roy turned and saw his son's son. Rodger had been standing there the whole time.

"You know about this crazy story?" Roy asked, shocked.

"Yes, sir, and it's true," Rodger said. "The man you see here came in peace to preserve and protect life just as you've taught me to do. He did what he says he did and he is what he says. Please do as he asks and think about it, Grandpa."

Stung by his grandson's words, overwhelmed by the momentous events, Roy slid his gun into the holster and straightened his jacket, rising from the chair. "Time to go," he said simply, looking the man in the eye. "If my grandchild is telling the truth, then I'll know where to find you—right here."

"Yes, Mr. Harris. I won't betray your trust. I'll be here."

Roy looked at Rodger, whose eyes were wet with tears, and he started toward the stairs. On the first step up, Roy paused, turned, and said to the stranger: "Is everything you sought when you started your journey as you think it ought to be?"

The stranger took the question in and thought for a few moments. He swallowed a lump in his throat, closed his eyes and he answered, "Yes," and his voice trembled when he spoke. Roy observed this and proceeded up the stairs, out of the house and across the street to Earl, who had finished canvassing the block and stood at the cul-de-sac admiring the view of downtown Los Angeles. "Roy, isn't it beautiful?" Earl said as more of a statement than a question, looking at the glow of the cityscape in the distance, surrounded by the blackness of hills, mountains and a faraway ocean. "Even after the sun sets, this is a city of angels."

Chapter 12: Reunion

Roy and Arlene Harris arrived home simultaneously, to find it still surrounded by media trucks and those feeding on the media frenzy. It was nearly two o'clock in the morning. As they each pulled into the driveway, the media camp stirred, floodlights flared up and on-air personalities went scurrying like rodents. None of the arrival was caught on camera.

One breathless blonde exhorted: "It appears that both husband and wife have come home in the wee hours of the morning. We had been aware that they'd left the house, though we do not yet know where they went. The couple arrived in separate cars a few minutes ago. We'll get the details of their late-night outing as soon as we have more information. Stay tuned."

Another said: "The retired police detective who married his murder victim's widow and the woman whose murdered husband was a United States senator—whom we now know was an accused pedophile and child sex trafficker—just came home. We're working on finding out where they've been."

So were they. Husband and wife, shielded in their mutual homecoming by the police officers who had erected a barrier and tarps to cover their carport, met in the kitchen.

"Out for a drive?" Roy asked his wife.

"Sort of," she said, still in the striped shirt she had on earlier in the day. "You, too?"

"No, not really. I was working with Earl on a security case. It went later than I thought it would. I ran into Rodger," he said flatly. "I met his physics professor. He's one of a kind."

Pouncing on what she considered good news, Arlene said: "You met the mysterious Dr. Manther? Did you get to see why he's a hero to our grandchild?"

"Yes, I did, and in the most extraordinary way. He gave me something to think about," Roy answered.

Arlene noticed something in the way her husband spoke tonight that was different than before. She was about to say something when he added, "And how are you, my dear wife? Have you anything to think about?"

Arlene almost collapsed at his question. "Do I. Oh, Roy. Everything with Jim and that awful woman was unknown to me—."

"Stop, Arlene," said her husband.

He went on: "I do not know what happened in your home before we met. I do not want to know unless it will help you and the kids be truer to yourselves. If it helps, I want to know. Not if it doesn't. So, don't tell me anything out of guilt, shame or fear. I want no part of you owning what isn't earned. I'm your husband. I love you."

She flung herself into his arms and her body moved in muffled gasps for air, life and love. When her sorrow had subsided, Arlene turned and rested her head on Roy's shoulder. After a few minutes in his arms, she spoke as if in prayer: "I always knew something was wrong. Even while we were dating. I'll tell you everything you need to know, Roy, and I'll get through this and sort things out. I want to spend the rest of my life helping Mike and Natalie sort things out, too. What happened was terrible." She turned her head and looked up at him, "It could have been worse."

The stranger had told him the same thing. "I think I understand," he said.

"I don't know anything about this sex trafficking ring, and I honestly thought he was using Eleanor Jones for campaign contributions. I had no idea they were involved. He was smooth, Roy, he could make me believe almost anything—."

"I know. He was a sociopath."

"When I found out what he did to the kids, I thought about telling someone. I went to the library and read volumes of books about abuse, and I researched how to parent abuse victims and I went to a therapist. I was weak and confused and afraid. I was not in my right mind. He was a U.S. senator and he made me feel small, and I wasn't sure I could do anything that would result in a positive outcome. Then he was killed. I've carried this with me for a long time. I've had to live with this." She added: "I am guilty."

Arlene turned to her husband. "I am also relieved now it's out in the open. It's time to make amends so I can enjoy what's left of my life and make sure I've atoned for what I've done to my children. They deserved a better mother than me."

He didn't disagree. He listened.

"I apologize, Roy. For you having to pay the price for my worst mistake. It's different today than it was in 1959. I would have told someone if I'd known what I know now. I couldn't talk about it then. And later, when I could have, so much time had already passed. It seemed better to leave it alone. I am sorry I didn't tell you. I have no right to ask for your forgiveness. But please think about forgiving me."

He took her by the shoulders and then cupped his large hands on her small, thin jaw. He looked deep into her eyes and, in slow, even words, he said: "I forgive you, Arlene."

Her eyes closed and he felt her exhale.

"Do you know where I was?" She asked after a few minutes. "I drove to Parker Center to meet Eleanor Jones."

He tried not to show his shock and alarm.

"I know—I know—it was stupid of me. I'd talked to her attorney and arranged the whole thing to happen in secret, no press, just woman to woman. I wanted to find out what had happened and tell her to confess everything or I knew people who could have her killed in jail. Or worse."

She looked up at him again. "And I do."

He nodded.

"But halfway there, I realized that I would only want to reach across and grab her and bash her face in. Of course, at some point during the drive I realized that all I could gain from the visit is a breach of the case against her. So, I headed over to the lake at Echo Park and I sat for a while."

Arlene hung her head. "I sat there watching people, feeding the ducks, looking at the city. I thought for a long time and I cried and cried until there wasn't anything left. I made an important realization, Roy. Until you came along, we were all on our way to dying or we were already dead. You brought our family together— you and your love. Your ability to be serious and enjoy life and pursue justice gave me and the kids a deeper love and stronger safety than we ever would have known. That's when I knew that if Jim hadn't been murdered, I would have been dead. The kids, too. Or not exactly alive."

She pulled him closer and hung on tight and they were silent for several minutes. Then Arlene Harris softly but evenly told her husband what he probably needed to hear: "I'm frankly glad someone killed my husband. He was a monster. I don't know who did it or why, but he got what he deserved and, in a way, I owe the person that ended James Warner's life my life—he gave me another shot, a new beginning. Whoever killed James Warner set me free. Thank God you were there."

She looked up at him again. This time, the tears were in his eyes. "I'm glad I've been your wife for 50 years. I love you. Please have me back."

He took her hand, kissing it gently. "One step at a time," he said. "Get some rest."

With that, Roy sent exhausted Arlene off to bed. He walked into his home office and picked up the phone, dialing Earl.

The conversation was brief and purposeful. He calmly explained to his former partner that he was in possession of a gun owned by Eleanor Jones which had matched the ballistics report and other corroborating evidence at the crime scene of Senator Warner's homicide. He told Earl he'd found the weapon buried nearby after receiving an anonymous tip and that the gun was the murder weapon and Earl should bring charges against Eleanor Jones for the murder of James Warner. Then, he asked Earl for a single favor: file the report and do not ask me any questions. Earl knew that his partner had his reasons. Eleanor Jones would be charged with pre-meditated murder in the first degree.

He then slipped out back by the pool and walked over to a veteran police officer who was posted to guard the property from the press. Roy had known the cop for 31 years and he asked him for a favor. Within 15 minutes, an up-and-coming public relations officer appeared and Roy told her that he had information that the press would love to have. The young communications officer eagerly listened to what she heard; that Eleanor Jones, the depraved social climber arrested for child sex trafficking, known throughout Washington, D.C, and Hollywood, who had been collaborating with Warner, had murdered her depraved partner in a jealous rage over his sexual attraction to children. Her ex-husband would, under questioning, corroborate that Eleanor Jones was also a pedophile and that she had been having an affair with the senator. The PR cop waddled away from the conversation toward the press tent and Roy knew the story would lead the local and national news cycle by sunrise.

It did—only sooner. Within a couple of hours, the media was breaking the news that charity maven Eleanor Jones was a pedophile and sex trafficker in cahoots with another pedophile and sex trafficker, and that she would soon be charged for the first-degree murder of James Warner.

By then, 5 a.m. Pacific time, retired Det. Roy Harris was safely in the passenger seat of an unmarked police car with his veteran cop buddy on the freeway heading toward Pasadena. The car pulled up to Dr. Manther's house on the hill and slowed to park at the curb. Roy opened the door while it was still moving. He stepped out and walked up to the front door. This time, he didn't ring the bell. He turned the knob and walked right in. He looked to the left and saw Rodger sprawled out on the living room sofa, sound asleep. It was pitch black except for a thin strip of light near the floorboard. It illuminated the house with a soft dim light. Roy moved toward the basement staircase, but he stopped when he heard a whisper.

"Here, Detective Harris." The voice said. It was Dr. Manther's. He was behind him the whole time. "Let's go into my private quarters."

Moving to the other end of the modern house, which was white with stone and slate features, floors and furniture, they came to a long, narrow office lined with bookshelves that opened into a lush garden patio. "Here," Dr. Manther said, "please make yourself comfortable." They stepped through paned glass doors to the patio which overlooked the mountains to the north. The cop and the scientist took their seats.

Dr. Manther—aka Jeff Thurman—looked at Roy Harris and held his gaze. "So, what have you decided?"

"That you are right," came the reply.

The doctor smiled as he listened. "Go on."

"I'm having her charged with murder," Roy explained in a low voice, as if talking to a comrade on a stakeout. "She'll probably be held without bond until the trial." He added: "I'm sorry about your Natalie."

He looked into the doctor's eyes, which pierced the darkness. What he saw made him feel better. The policeman felt as if he'd looked into the eyes of an angelic avenger. He swiftly stood up and extended his hand.

"May I know your name?"

Dr. Manther, rising to meet him, gripping his hand in a firm shake, gave the slightest hint of a smile in the corner of his mouth. "Call me Jeff," he answered. "Jeff Thurman."

"A pleasure to know you, Mr. Thurman."

"Call me Jeff," he said. "I feel as if I know you."

"I'd like to know how that feels," Roy replied. "I'd like to feel as if I know you, too."

"There isn't time," Jeff said, "not this time." He saw a quizzical look on Roy's face and explained, "I've been shuttling back and forth between timelines and there's been some sort of breach or issue that I don't have a fix on yet. I have to leave here and investigate with my assistant, who's lost touch with me—it's a long story—and establish exactly what's happened. The science of this approach is new and developing."

"Is Rodger involved?"

"Only in studying and testing my theory, not in any live experiments. He knows enough to assist me, but I don't think he knows enough to transport on his own," Jeff said. "He knows that I'm here to make things right. Your grandson is enterprising. He reminds me of myself when I was young."

"What will you do now?" Roy asked.

"Go home. Try to fix what may be wrong in the present—my present—and move on with my life." He sounded almost cheerful, Roy thought, and if Jeff hadn't been looking down, he might have believed he was happy. Roy turned toward the glass wall, as the first suggestion of daylight rose from the east, and he started to leave.

He asked: "Will you do me one favor?"

"Yes, of course."

"Will you pick up my daughter at the airport?"

The question hung between them for a moment, until Roy said, "Her flight from Hong Kong landed 10 minutes ago." He added, with a slight smile: "Jeff, it's right on time."

Roy exited the patio without another word, as though presuming an affirmative answer, and said, without turning around, "Asian Air flight 515." Roy was out of the house, down the driveway, and getting into the police car parked at the curb. By the time he was gone, Jeff Thurman was halfway to his own car, having scribbled a note to Rodger, and soon he was heading toward the airport.

Early pre-dawn travelers moved in throngs as the voice over the loudspeaker made new and frequent announcements about air terminal security, flight delays and baggage claim rules. The new international terminal was a shining domed glass structure with gleaming metal beams, accents and supports. The latest announcement caught Natalie Warner Stefano's immediate attention.

"Will passenger Natalie Stefano please meet her party at the Asian Air guest lounge on the top level?"

She had been one of the last passengers off the flight from Hong Kong and had been waiting in the terminal's baggage area when she first heard the voiceover. Dressed in a smart blue traveling suit, the slender young wife and dancer wondered who had come to meet her at the airport. She knew that her father usually paid for the taxi when she arrived home from her travels. Mike was on a tour of duty in the Pacific. Rodger would already be working at this early hour. Who could it be? Natalie wondered. Was Anthony in town? Had Daddy sent one of the officers from the home security detail? With family secrets and new developments about her blood father's sordid life, her mind raced and she wondered whether the announcement was some sort of trap set by the media—staked out at the airline lounge to snap her photo and paste it all over the world, linking a Tantham Ballet ballerina and inventor's wife to a dead senator's salacious and revolting crimes.

Her cell phone rang as she walked to the escalator.

Natalie looked at the display and saw that it was her father calling.

"Dad? Everything OK?" She answered.

"Fine here, my dear," he said, more tenderly than usual, she thought. "I'm calling to let you know that I've asked a family friend, who you won't remember, to pick you up."

"Oh, that explains it—I'm on my way to meet him now, Dad. What's his name? Is he a cop I know?"

"No, but he's one of the good guys, Natalie. Call him Jeff."

Natalie thanked Roy and hung up as she rode the long, wide escalator to the top of the domed terminal. She looked straight up and could still see the twinkling stars against the sky amid the dome's muted nightlights. At the top, she stepped into a red and black themed airline club lounge. It looked like something out of an Art Deco set—curves, glass and sleek lines.

Surrounded by the glass dome with a view of every international takeoff and landing—including those flying overhead—the airline lounge was located at top of the dome, seemingly at the center of all the air traffic. The morning's first sunrays came through the dome's metal and glass in beams of blinding gold through a prism.

"Welcome," greeted the host at the door. "May I take your bag?"

"No, thank you—I was paged and I'm here to meet my party. I'm the passenger Natalie Stefano."

"Yes, Mrs. Stefano, we've been expecting you," said an elegant, older gentleman. "Your husband is here. He's seated and waiting at booth 488."

She peered over the counter past the host and caught a glimpse of a man's square jaw in profile—before she fully heard what had been said. She turned without looking and asked: "Did you say 'husband'?"

But the host was gone, disappearing into the bustling lounge, which was milling with dozens of travelers, pilots and airline personnel. Natalie slowly moved into the lounge, spotting the number 488 on a gold-metal plate on the side of a long, curved booth directly beneath the dome. Sunbursts pierced the darkness in the dining room at this exact spot. Natalie paused for a moment to take in the splendor. A man gracefully stepped up to her.

"Mrs. Stefano." He said. "My name is Jeff."

She was taken by his height, voice and manner. "Jeff," she said, searching her mind for anyone she knew named Jeff, "how do you do?"

They exchanged a handshake; he took her carry-on bag and they slowly sat down at the same time.

"Would you like a drink?" He asked.

Travel-haggard Natalie looked like she thought that was a marvelous idea. "A Pinot Grigio, please."

He ordered one for her and Champagne for himself. "Make that two glasses, please."

"Oh," she asked as the waitress left, "what are we celebrating?"

"Life," he said. "I've known your family for some time, though it's a long story which I don't have time to tell this morning."

She was puzzled, and she was intrigued. "I must have been very young," she said, leaning in, "my memory is good and my family is pretty close, so I don't know why I don't remember you."

Jeff looked her over. Natalie, his wife, the same woman he'd first seen gliding across the stage like a ray of light unleashed to music—the woman whose body he'd buried—was right here before him, yet somehow, she was not the same woman. She didn't belong to him—not that Natalie ever really did, he thought, appraising her as she fluffed her chestnut brown hair— but she looked as though she belonged to someone.

She noticed him looking.

"Are you a cop?" She asked dryly.

"No," he answered.

Drinks were served. She sampled her wine, nodded to the waitress, and there was a crystal glass of Champagne waiting for her.

"Here's to your life—well lived," he said, raising his glass. Jeff drank from his glass and resumed his watchful gaze. She raised her own, drank and watched him watching her.

"I think I must be missing something."

Jeff chuckled. "Not really. I knew you at a different time, that's all. I am glad to see you've turned out so well. Are you happy?"

"On most days, yes," she answered easily. "Especially when I come home to California. Frank—that's my husband—is still closing his deal overseas. He'll be home soon. I miss him already. But I want to see my parents. They need me right now."

"They may need you less than you think," he said.

Natalie drew back, as if he had assumed too much.

"Look," he said. "I know everything, Mrs. Stefano. So, does your dad. It all came out while you were gone. "

She looked at him blankly, thinking: *he couldn't possibly know about my past—whoever he is—no one knows but Mike and Mom—we kept it a secret.*

Jeff continued: "It's alright. Don't ask how I know. It doesn't matter. Just know that I do. Your parents and Mike are fine. So is Rodger. Yes, he knows, too. So, please let it go. None of it matters now. What counts is that you're here," he said, adding quietly, "and that you're happy."

Natalie acquired a look of wonder on her face, as if she were in the presence of an angel. She was on the verge of saying something, when the visitor anticipated her and said: "Never mind who I am—or who I used to be. I am a friend of your family. I care about you. That's all that matters now."

He finished his Champagne, picked up the check and looked at his wristwatch. "We should be going," he said.

She noticed the fine fabrics of his clothes, the elegance of his wristwatch, the confidence of his physical movements. She asked: "Do we have time to finish our celebration?"

Jeff couldn't bear to look at her in this moment—he might have wanted more than he had a right to, so he focused on a jet climbing overhead above the dome. He thought of Mabus, the time machine and how this moment came to be. He started to realize something.

They sat wordlessly in the newborn sunrise under the curved glass, amid comings and goings of hurried travelers striving to make connections in time. She smiled at her new friend—whom she would never see again—while sipping her wine as he admired the woman she had chosen to become. In spite of his efforts, she had been stained by James Warner. Jeff hadn't been able to stop it in time. But sitting across from the woman he once loved, he could see that she hadn't been ruined—Jeff had stopped that—and he knew in that moment that she had overcome the damage and her life would not be tragic.

Beneath waning stars and emerging sunlight, the avenger who had once been her husband and the dancer who had once been his wife rose from their places to end what one of them knew was their first and last reunion. He took her hand in his and her bag in his other hand and they departed as they had arrived: brave strangers to one another who seemed oddly together yet apart.

Jeff's re-connection to Natalie ended there at the terminal really, for the drive to her parents' home was quiet and formal and sealed like a final good-bye. He focused on the road, the cars and traffic in front of him. She thought about her future with Frank and pushed aside the excitement of the encounter with a mysterious visitor. They arrived a block from the house, where Jeff had asked Roy to have an armed officer meet them to escort her discreetly to her destination.

"Good-bye, Natalie," he said, dropping the Mrs. and meaning what he said. "I've enjoyed seeing you one more time."

Natalie lifted her chin. "Good-bye, Jeff," she replied, then she said, "and God bless you for whatever it is that you did." She started to leave with the policeman but turned back once more to look up to him, "I think we both know there is more than I can say." It was both a dare and a plea and she'd said it quickly in a whisper. She then reached up to his face, stroked it and, sensing she should stop there, abruptly turned and walked away. Jeff Thurman watched Natalie, her escort with luggage in tow, until her trim figure in blue disappeared around the bend. The spot where she left his view hung in his mind for a moment, her silhouette burnished in his memory. Then, he let it go. She was gone.

EPILOGUE

I am told that Christmastime at the Harris home that season was especially joyful.

Mike and Patrice arrived on leave after some excitement at sea involving their vessel in what some suspect is a satellite-driven security breach during a solar storm. They're visiting Rodger, who I've learned is developing a microchip intended for convicted perverts and some new experiment that improves upon one of Dr. Manther's—Jeff's—contraptions.

Frank and Natalie are celebrating his new business in Hong Kong—and they're trying to conceive. Natty opened a dance school in Arcadia. She's opening three more next year in Tarzana, Baldwin Hills and Simi Valley. She's bringing Anthony on to manage the schools. Roy and Arlene sold the house and moved to a condo in Century City, where Roy works as a security executive and Arlene works with adult children of sexual abuse.

Everyone knows what happened to Mike and Natalie as children—though Roy and Rodger think it's best for no one else to know about Jeff's mission in time—and, on this particular Christmas, the Harris family is giving themselves the gift of love—a love which will someday heal deep wounds.

During Jeff's absence, I lost my life to old age—really, just wear and tear—though not before leaving a projection of Jeff's future in the form of a diary, a version of which you're reading now. Before I depart, I've created a painting of Jeff with Tugs. It's a favorite memory of the boy genius, who became a man who changed the world matching the work of his mind with an extraordinary sense of play. My dying is not painful as I write this. I feel amazingly alive, if ready to bid my life adieu, good about my life well lived—and I must say I've had a wonderful time.

I know Jeff will love again. You see, what he realized on that morning with Natalie is that the meaning of his journey is his own salvation—not exactly or exclusively Natalie's—and, since I'd figured out a few things about that temporal dilation theory and the machine, I know that when I depart, Jeff will find his way back to being his best, living in the bliss of his own rich life.

No matter how damaged, or how charged with punishment the scroll, in the words of William Ernest Henley, Jeff turned himself right and led the way to a whole, virtuous life. He is already well into the rest of his life. I'd still like to see that, mind you. What a life it is.

But I've done my part in parenting Jeff Thurman. His life belongs to him.

Whatever else is wrong with the world—and the world is very much in turmoil—I have come to learn that that's what being a man means; to live as if you own it, because you do. The sun goes up. The sun goes down. It is man who makes the world dark, or enlightened, and gives the world its splendor, direction and glory.